AF751663

Yvette Poshoglian

Dear Greta

PUFFIN BOOKS

PUFFIN BOOKS

UK | USA | Canada | Ireland | Australia
India | New Zealand | South Africa | China

Penguin
Random House
Australia

Penguin Random House Australia is part of the Penguin Random House group of companies whose addresses can be found at global.penguinrandomhouse.com.

First published by Puffin Books, an imprint of Penguin Random House Australia Pty Ltd, in 2022

Copyright © Yvette Poshoglian 2022

The moral right of the author has been asserted.

All rights reserved. No part of this publication may be reproduced, published, performed in public or communicated to the public in any form or by any means without prior written permission from Penguin Random House Australia Pty Ltd or its authorised licensees.

This is a work of fiction. Although it references real-life people and places, events and foundations, their relation to this story is purely fictitious, as are all the characters. No part of this work is endorsed by Greta Thunberg.

Cover illustrations and design by Astred Hicks, Design Cherry
Internal design and typesetting by Midland Typesetters, Australia
Internal images: emojis © popicon/Shutterstock.com, bullet points and chapter heading wavy line © Neti.OneLove/Shutterstock.com

Printed and bound in Australia by Griffin Press, an accredited ISO AS/NZS 14001 Environmental Management Systems printer

NATIONAL LIBRARY OF AUSTRALIA

A catalogue record for this book is available from the National Library of Australia

ISBN 978 1 76 104378 9

Penguin Random House Australia uses papers that are natural and recyclable products, made from wood grown in sustainable forests. The logging and manufacture processes are expected to conform to the environmental regulations of the country of origin.

penguin.com.au

FSC
www.fsc.org
MIX
Paper | Supporting responsible forestry
FSC® C018684

For Greta, grandmothers and Greenpeace

SAVE FILE TAB 1

Alice Boghosian

Class 6O – Library writing project

Thursday 28 January 2021

~~Dear Ms Greta Thunberg, Sweden~~
~~Dear Greta Thunberg,~~
Dear Greta,

I'm going to call you *Greta* because this whole 'write to your hero' project that Mrs Malouf, our school librarian, has given us feels like something kids would have done in the olden days – who writes letters any more? Does anyone read them? We're both teenagers – well, technically, ***you're*** a teenager and I'm *going to be* a teenager soon – so it seems silly to write to you in such an old-fashioned way.

At least Mrs Malouf's finally agreed to turn this writing assignment into *emails* . . .

I hope it's okay that I call you *Greta*. Calling you *Ms Thunberg* (which Mrs Malouf recommended) doesn't seem right.

I didn't get to choose you, Greta, and I'm not saying you're *not* a hero of mine – it's just that I don't know enough about you to call you a hero. And don't take this the wrong way, but, on my hero list, I'm not sure that you'd be in the Top 3. My Top 3 actually looks like this:

1. Queenie Q – the social media queen who is only 14 and has 22 million followers and posts pictures of her puppy dressed up in costumes
2. Maddy Proud – captain of my favourite netball team, the Sydney Swifts
3. Taylor Swift – because she's Taylor Swift, okay?

I'm willing to do the research on you, though, Greta, so stand by.

This all happened because Jayden Tutai ran into me and spilled his chocolate milk all over my school dress. Now, I'm wearing a scratchy old uniform from the seconds rack in the Uniform

Shop that smells like mothballs and hangs past my knees. I've been forced to sit next to Jayden and I've been forced to write to you, the only hero left in the basket that Mrs Malouf had put all the heroes' names into.

Jayden is stressing out next to me, and he got his actual hero – James Tamou. I can see out of the corner of my eye that he's stuck on *Dear Mr Tamou.* His face is all scrunched up, and he looks like he might actually be sick. Surely he can think of something to say to the captain of his favourite footy team, the Tigers, who he never shuts up about. Even *I* know enough about NRL to write a couple of sentences – my parents have been taking us to Tigers matches for years in the hope that they win another premiership.

'Isn't it wonderful that you got *Greta* to write to?' Mrs Malouf smiles at me with glee. Suddenly, she's hovering at my side.

I think it's cruel to give assignments on the first day of school. But I say, 'I guess.'

'Hmmm,' she says, sniffing. 'Do I detect . . . mothballs?' She's looking at me, quizzically.

Jayden coughs, trying to cover a laugh, so I shove him in the ribs with my elbow.

'It's a long story,' I say, and sigh dramatically, throwing Jayden a death stare.

'I'm sorry, *Bogus*,' he says. 'I mean, *Mothballs*.' As if it's not bad enough that I had one horrible nickname, it seems I now have two. I've been trying to dodge my nickname for years. It's not my fault that *Boghosian* kind of sounds like *Bogus*. To some people (not me).

Kind regards (Mrs Malouf suggested that I write that to say goodbye),
Alice Boghosian
Melwood Public School
Australia

PS – I know we're supposed to just save these files in our portfolio folder, but what's the point of writing letters or emails if you don't actually *send* them to someone? I think I've tracked down your email address, Greta, and copied my 'letter' into an email. This is coming your way.

SAVE FILE TAB 2

Alice Boghosian

Class 6O - Library writing project

Friday 29 January 2021

Dear Greta (again),

It's Alice here from Melwood Public School library. I found your email address (I think) so I hope you don't mind receiving my 'letters'.

I did read that you are developing a foundation, but I couldn't find any more information about it, despite putting on my internet detective hat. I can't imagine being seventeen and having assistants and a foundation named after me to help me with my plans for the world!

If I had a foundation, The Alice Boghosian Foundation, I would definitely have two assistants, maybe three. I'm not sure what my foundation would be for, however . . . The things that I am passionate about would be too funny to start a super serious 'foundation' about.

There are things that I want, of course: glossy, straight hair instead of my wild curls, which I can't tame even with a hundred anti-frizz serums (and Mum won't buy me a straightener); to start a TikTok channel with my friends, Anh and Sami, where we show off our dance moves (currently put on hold because one of our dance members is down); to publish a book based only on text messages (sorry, Mrs Malouf!).

I think almost every form of communication today comes down to texting. For instance, a tennis ball emoji from Sami means *Do you want to meet at the handball courts at lunch?* Even Mum and Dad send messages using emojis. I reckon I've already written a whole book to Sami made up entirely of text messages. Sometimes, we can have a whole conversation using a single emoji – tops *two.* ☺ 🤗

Mrs Malouf was very firm, though. 'We are *writing,*' she paused on that special word, 'to very special people. People who are leaders in some way – leaders of the world, leaders in their community, you get the idea. Text messaging is not writing. Emojis are not forms of communication.'

'Is there an emoji for mothballs?' Jayden then asked.

I'm still considering kicking him under the table. For some reason, Mrs Malouf had ushered Jayden and I to this front table again for our second writing-project lesson, before I could follow Sami to sit with her. My response to him: 

But back to you, Greta. From my googling, I know you've changed the world, but before I write any more to you about climate change, which is your specialty, I need to do some research of my own. 

Kind regards/goodbye,
Alice Boghosian
Melwood Public School
Sydney, Australia

SAVE FILE TAB 3

Alice Boghosian

Class 6O - Library writing project

Monday 1 February 2021

Dear Greta,

Happy first of the month! It's now, technically, the second week of Year Six, but it will be the first full week for our classes in Year Six. I'm in 6O this year. Over the weekend, I realised that *my* email to you is probably just one of thousands that you receive every day – although I bet the others are from activists and climate-change warriors from all around the world. I'm probably more of a climate change 'investigator' at this stage, if I'm honest.

I want to do really well this year. I want to leave primary school on a high, and Mum has always said that I'm good at writing, so I'm giving this writing assignment my best shot. But apart from having a tiny *haiku* called *Spring Blossom* published in the school newsletter back in Year Three, I've never really written anything else. One thing that I am good at is typing and texting very quickly. Mum says it's because I always have a lot to say.

For this library project, we have to save our letters to folders for Mrs Malouf and our new class teacher Ms O'Rourke to read. Although I'm keeping a copy of each on my personal drive so that I can send them to you, as well. As I've already said, what's the point of writing to someone if you never actually press 'send'? I could also argue, what's the point if the someone doesn't write back . . .? But that's a one-sided conversation for another day.

Mrs Malouf has put pictures up of all the heroes for our writing assignment, so I can see your face, Ash Barty's and others as I write this.

I love hanging out in the library. There have been a lot of quality times hanging on the beanbags in the senior fiction area. I found some of my favourite books in here – like *The Diary of a Young Girl*, which is sometimes known as *The Diary of Anne Frank*. She didn't live to experience the impact her words had on the world. The impact they still have . . . Sometimes, at night, when I look around my bedroom just before switching off the light, I try to imagine a whole family living in this one room. How did Peter and Anne's families live in such a tiny place for so long? The fear of being caught by the Nazis must have been so overwhelming. Sometimes, if I think too much about it, I really scare myself and have to turn the light back on. Anne couldn't even do that.

The library has a big window that looks out onto the quadrangle and is right under the air-conditioning, making it the perfect place to be on the extra-hot days. Today's one of those days, but I'm stuck again at the front bank of computers where there's no window and no air-conditioning, just the heavy tip-tapping of Jayden on his keyboard and the small sighs of what sound like pain from the new girl Hannah.

Hannah just moved here from South Korea. She hides under her fringe, and has a way of tucking her neck into her shoulder so that she doesn't have to make eye contact. I know her English is good, as she's always able to answer the teachers' questions (even if it's in a very quiet voice). But she doesn't really talk to us. I've tried all the things: making eye contact, sighing loudly and even whistling, but I'm not getting any response from her. I just get annoyed sounds from Jayden next to me. But we've had three library lessons together now, and we haven't said that much to each other. And since it seems like we'll be spending a lot of time here in the library, I need to be able to chat to someone . . .

'Who did you get as your hero?' I whisper, trying to start a conversation. But again, Hannah ducks behind her fringe and goes red.

This is depressing. I want things to go back to how they were last year. In Year Five, we used to just choose a book each and read it on beanbags, or Mrs Malouf would read one of her favourite books out loud to us. Last term, she read us *Once* by Morris Gleitzman, which meant that I then had to borrow the entire series just to find out what happens to Felix. (I think you'd like those books, Greta – strong hero, takes action against the odds . . .)

'Beyoncé,' Hannah whispers suddenly.

She got *Beyoncé*. Why did I have to get you, Greta? I can't ask you about being rich, making music and being a complete superstar. I would have known exactly what to write to Beyoncé.

Things are going to get better, right?

Yours sincerely, (Mrs Malouf also recommended this as a way of signing off on letters.)
Alice Boghosian
Melwood Public School
Australia

SAVE FILE TAB 4

Alice Boghosian

Class 6O - Library writing project

Tuesday 2 February 2021

Dear Greta,

How many people write to you every day? Do world leaders just pick up the phone? Do they have your mobile number? What sort of things do they ask? Is it for advice on climate change? Is it information on your latest adventures? I'm sure you're busy . . .

Do you find it overwhelming being a leader at such a young age to so many people around the world? You've achieved so much in your life already. My major plans involve getting through my last year of primary school, and somehow not interacting at all with my older sister, Annie. Oh, and leaving some kind of impression on Melwood Public before I go to high school.

It sounds like you get on really well with your sister, Beata. From what I've read about you so far, you and Beata seem to have joined forces to convince your parents to give up meat and flying. My sister and I barely speak to each other, and so there's no way we could convince our parents to do anything, let alone something as serious as giving up meat or flying on planes. Annie is a super-annoying sister, and she just thinks she's really important because she's at high school.

And you have two dogs: Roxy and Moses. The closest that I come to having a pet is living next door to Mr Chang's nesting pigeons. Mum and Dad won't let us get a pet – I'd be up for a dog, cat or even a parakeet, but my parents won't budge.

Have I mentioned my mum and dad to you before now? Mum is an artist at heart, but she works as a medical receptionist. She basically runs the surgery. I know she would much rather be painting, or re-upholstering furniture which is her latest passion. Dad is a water scientist. They both work really hard all the time, and this year I want to make them happy by getting good results and leaving my mark on Melwood Public School.

The internet is overwhelming, but I don't need to tell you that. A simple Google search of your name brings up 23.5 million results. A lot of it seems to be adults hating on you (shouldn't they be the grown-ups?), which is horrible. The world is rubbish when adults pick on kids. I reckon it's because everything *you* say seems to show them up.

I googled myself, and I found a picture of me and my family at the opening of our local park in 2017 (my hair was really frizzy that day), and then a picture of me at a soccer match. Although, I left soccer behind after just one season in favour of netball, and so if anyone googled Alice Boghosian they really wouldn't get the full story at all.

I've just made the mistake of looking up my sister. Annie Boghosian has over a hundred actual entries. Winner of the Science Fair, runner-up for the National Science Prize, winner of the Young Achiever's Award from Whitlam High School 2020.

Whatever you do, don't google yourself, Greta. Maybe the only thing worse than having too much about you online is having nothing at all.

Bye for now,
Alice Boghosian

SAVE FILE TAB 5

Alice Boghosian

Class 6O – Library writing project

Wednesday 3 February 2021

Dear Greta,

Some of the stuff you can easily find on the internet are things you've said that became famous. One of your most famous quotes is that our house is on fire. Like, the whole world. Here in Australia, we all feel like that every summer.

Black Summer was different, though, Greta. It was one of the scariest things I've ever been through, and the fires around Sydney weren't even near our house in Melwood, but the smoke was! The smell of barbecues being lit reminds me of waking up every day and seeing brown bushfire sky pushing down on us that summer. I can still taste the bitter smell of smoke in the air. The sky, the smoke, and the horrible smell that got into your clothes, stayed in your nose and burned the back of your throat. It went on for months and months, and people and animals literally lost their homes, and now we have animal species that we don't even think will recover, they're so endangered after the bushfires.

And now it's happening in other countries, too – in America and Canada. When I was in Year Four, I did a project on the fires in the Amazon. Now, it looks like Greece and Spain are on fire, too. It's everywhere, just like you said.

I can't believe how many articles there are about you online and how many comments people post around everything that you do and say. The strangest thing I found is that right below your official TIME magazine 2019 Person of the Year Google result is a thread debating whether or not you are actually an Australian actor named *Estella Renee*. That's why you can't believe everything on the internet – it's fake news half the time. Should I call you Estella from now on?

Names can be tricky. Just take mine. *Boghos* is the Armenian form of *Paul*. All Armenian names end in *–ian*. It means 'son of'. What if the names meant 'daughter of'? That would be cool. The world might be a different place if girls ran the world, like Beyoncé says.

The most famous Armenians in the world are the Kardashians, and I'm not sure if that's a good or bad thing. Armenians, by the way, excel at weightlifting in the Olympics, which gives you an indication of their collective core body strength and strong necks as a people. I guess the Swedish are good at Winter Olympics stuff, like sledding and skiing.

I try to imagine my life as *Alice Paulson* in an alternative universe, but there's no use doing that. I'm me. My grandmother changed her Armenian name, Vartouhi, to Rose because it was easier when she came to Australia. But I don't think I would ever change my name, and I hope I don't have to.

I do need to try and get the class to stop calling me *Mothballs*, thanks to Jayden Tutai. But no one listens to me. I can't get them to stop calling me names any more than I could get the world to change what they are doing to save the environment.

Mrs Malouf is giving us her wind-things-up signal, so I'm typing as fast as I can go. Sami and I have organised to get to the handball courts before any of the other Year Sixes get them, so I need to hurry.

I keep making the same spello.

Did you know that if you type *Greta* really fast, it spells out *Great*? How cool is that?

See ya later/kind regards,
Alice Boghosian

SAVE FILE TAB 6

Alice Boghosian

Class 6O – Library writing project

Thursday 4 February 2021

Dear Greta,

I'm still being made to sit at the first computer bank with Jayden for our library writing lessons, which are going to be every day this term. I don't know why Mrs Malouf is doing this to me but she has decided to glue us all to the exact same seats where we began this assignment. And you know what a disaster that was . . . is. I work so much better sitting next to Sami! I can't stand being around Jayden.

But if I put my chair at an angle, get Hannah to move her head slightly, and then twist my head around my computer, I can see Sami.

Sami isn't exactly overjoyed with library lessons at the moment, either. That's because she got

Ash Barty, the tennis star. I love Ash Barty, and I actually know about tennis . . . it would have been good if I could have given her *you*, and she had given me *Ash.*

'I had to google *Wimbledon* today,' Sami said, at recess. 'It's not exactly big in Iran.' Sami lived in Iran before moving to Australia when she was six, and came to our school in Year One.

'How's your Greta writing going?' she asked me.

'Still researching,' I said. I didn't feel like telling her all about the massive emails I've been sending you, Greta.

'One thing that Greta Thunberg does is stand up for what she believes in,' said Sami. 'I've seen that documentary on her.'

Note to self: watch the documentary on you. I've been thinking about standing up for things. And standing up to people. So maybe you and your documentary will inspire me! You definitely do what you think is right . . .

'I can't even stand up to Jayden for calling me *Bogus* since kindy,' I said. 'Now, it's *Mothballs.*'

Honestly, I'm annoyed with myself. If someone were picking on Sami, I'd fight that person without gloves on. But telling Jayden and his mates to stop?

If I just don't draw attention to it, maybe it will go away . . .

I'm sorry I'm not as strong as you, Greta.

Bye,
Alice Boghosian

SAVE FILE TAB 7

Alice Boghosian

Class 6O - Library writing project

Friday 5 February 2021

Dear Greta,

Yay! I'm not stuck with Jayden and Hannah-not-saying-anything in this lesson. Because Anh is with me, here at the front computer bank. I just checked my last letter to you and realised I haven't told you about Anh yet.

When I say 'Anh is here with me', I mean 'Anh the telerobot'. Real Anh is at home in bed this term – the Black Summer fires were really hard on Anh and her lungs, so now she has to be careful all the time. She has to check the air quality on a daily basis, and when there's smoke around it's really difficult for her – but robo-Anh (which is the next best thing) comes to school with us. Anh is my other best friend, who I may not have mentioned, because she only started back at school this week. It's already made Year Six *way* better.

Having the robot means Anh can steer it around the school and still come to lessons, even while she's home in bed. She controls the robot by using her iPad. The robot itself has wheels and a long pole up to its 'face' (an iPad screen). I'm responsible for making sure Anh's robot is charged every day. And so, just before hometime, I take Anh's robot to Cortez's room (Cortez is our Year Six adviser. No one ever calls him Mr Cortez), where there's a battery plate that charges the robot overnight.

Anh is the third side of our triangle of friendship with Sami and me. The three of us have been best friends since Year Three. None of us have ever had a fight. (Well, none that I know about between Sami and Anh, but I definitely haven't had a fight with either of them.)

Anh's always had bad asthma, but lately it has been getting worse and, in summer, she has to be really careful on smoky days. On the worst days, Anh needs to stay hooked up to her oxygen machine, and I know she just doesn't feel like using the robot at those times. I don't blame her. I've tried to imagine how difficult it would be, to be stuck in bed and unable to breathe properly. The selfish part of me secretly thinks it would be great because my sister would have to wait on me and bring me snacks whenever I asked, but being able to breathe is pretty important, and I wouldn't give that away.

When Anh is okay, though, I call it an 'Anh Day', and Cortez sets the robot free from the charging dock. Anh takes control of it, and the robot becomes Anh herself. When she's whizzing along corridors, it even has her school jumper draped around it. Everyone in the whole school made a pact to treat the robot itself as . . . *Anh.* Everyone says hi when they can, and talks to her as if she's in the room. It wasn't easy to talk to a screen in the beginning, but we all got over it. Sometimes, visitors to the school don't understand what's happening, and they laugh or get embarrassed. Usually adults.

Cortez switched around the Year Five and Six classrooms especially for us. Normally, Year Six classrooms are upstairs, but this year they're all on the ground floor. So now, Anh can wheel everywhere with us to all the Year Six classrooms, the canteen, the library – and even the toilet blocks, which she tried out once. We all agreed she never actually needed to do that again.

'I got Malala to write to,' says Anh. 'Do you remember what happened to her?' she asks me, her face peering out from the screen. 'She was just standing up for girls to go to school in Pakistan,' Anh says. 'Girls like us.'

She means Malala Yousafzai. We studied her book in Year Four. The full story of what happened to Malala suddenly hits me. I wince, feeling a physical reaction. 'She was shot, wasn't she?' I look around the library. Why would it be so wrong to let girls go to school? I find it hard to understand why girls would be so threatening to adults.

'And she never stopped campaigning for girls,' says Anh. 'Even after all that. She is the youngest person to have won the Nobel Peace Prize. She's twenty-four now . . . she's done so much!'

'Girls are powerful, full stop,' I say. 'I mean, Greta was really young when she started protesting, and wasn't Malala only fifteen when she was protesting in Pakistan?'

I think about this, and how, between us, Anh, Sami and I could be a powerful force, too. A rush surges through me. Could we change the world, as well? For a small moment, it feels entirely possible. When I think about all the amazing girls, you and Malala in particular, it seems like anything is possible.

I'm just about to say something wise and powerful to Anh, but something stings me in the face.

'OW!'

I turn around, rubbing my cheek. Jayden is laughing his head off. Lance actually looks a bit embarrassed.

The elastic band he flicked at me is somewhere on the floor. Anh missed the whole thing because her camera was pointed in a different direction.

'Haha, Mothballs!'

Surely these stupid nicknames will wear off, won't they?

Yours in hope,
Alice Boghosian

SAVE FILE TAB 8

Alice Boghosian

Class 6O - Library writing project

Sunday 7 February 2021

Dear Greta,

I found a photo of you and Malala together when you went to England. It's made me think more about both of you, and how we instantly know you both by just your first names, 'Greta' and 'Malala'. You're both deservedly famous because, when you've seen something wrong, you've acted. And still do. You stand up for what you believe in (and, for Malala, it had terrible consequences).

What did you both talk about? I would have loved to have heard that conversation! Because it might help me deal with a few pesky 'issues' in my life. While they are not world emergencies, they sometimes feel just as huge to me!

The School Strike for Climate Change website that you must have helped set up recommends that children of the world:

- Hold their own demonstrations
- Donate to organisations supporting climate change
- Write to the United Nations
- Send a message of support (Maybe these emails count?)

So, could these ideas help me with my Year Six woes? I've never been to a demonstration before, but it looks exciting, with the signs and the drumbeats and the people all united together for the same cause.

I would love to demonstrate against some of the things happening in my life at the moment – imagine holding up a protest sign in the library that reads 'I DO NOT WANT TO SIT NEXT TO JAYDEN TUTAI'. That would be hilarious! (I wonder who would join me . . .)

You won the Children's Peace Prize in 2019 . . .

maybe you could create some peace between me and Jayden? And between me and my sister Annie, who is impossible to talk to, whereas Jayden won't stop talking to me, calling me names.

This is the worst start to the year . . . ever.

Kind regards/please help!
Alice Boghosian

PS – I hope you don't mind me writing to you on the weekend!

SAVE FILE TAB 9

Alice Boghosian

Class 6O - Library writing project

Monday 8 February 2021

Hallå Greta,

- *Hallå* (I googled the Swedish translation today)
- *Ni hau* (This is *hello* in Chinese – we studied a bit of Mandarin in Year Four)
- *Parev* (Armenian)

My teacher Ms O'Rourke told us during Geography that she had been to Sweden, 'but only for a weekend'. She also told us about some of the other countries around Sweden, like Finland and Norway and Denmark, which, I learned, when you group them together are called *Scandinavia*. Ms O'Rourke said she'd backpacked in Europe and ended up in Copenhagen when she was younger, between finishing uni and teaching at her first school. (Melwood Public is her fourth.) No one in my family has been to Sweden, I'm pretty sure of that.

Sweden looks beautiful. I'm scrolling through pictures of beautiful wooden houses on the water in Stockholm. That is where I imagine you live. The closest thing I have to water views is the Melwood Wetland Reserve, which my dad has been working hard to save from being turned into a freeway exit. It's basically a muddy bog. The nearest thing to actual water is the Parramatta River (also a muddy brown), which is about twenty minutes away, or Sydney Harbour itself (definitely not brown and about fifty minutes away).

My street is pretty plain and boring; everyone on it lives in a house that looks exactly like the next. The only difference between our house and Mr Chang's next door is the two cement lions at his front gate. The houses used to be Defence Housing, but then our block got sold off to buyers a few years ago, and so Mum and Dad had the chance to buy our house.

All the houses are bordered by strips of nature, lined with grass (that never quite turns green). Mum calls our home *A Postmodern Monstrosity*, and Dad calls it *Our Postmodern Monstrosity* (whatever that means).

Our street is typical Melwood; a neat, boring place. Melwood is the kind of place that you drive through to get to somewhere more interesting, which is probably why it is perched alongside a freeway that flows in and out of Sydney, and is a gateway into the Blue Mountains (which aren't really blue, they only seem that way from a distance).

See ya,
Alice Boghosian

PS – Jayden and his mates have only called me *Mothballs* twice today, and *Bogus* once, so maybe things are looking up?

SAVE FILE TAB 10

Alice Boghosian

Class 6O - Library writing project

Monday 8 February 2021 (pm)

Dear Greta,

Normally before bed, I look at the pile of books on my bedside table, mostly ignore them, and do some stuff on Mum's iPad (which she has loaned me this year – but only for school work). And tonight's no different. There's a lot I want to tell you before I get to school to write again in the library, so I hope you don't mind me emailing you from bed.

My room is my favourite place in the world. I have stacks of my favourite magazine, *Kookie*, neatly piled next to my bed. I was allowed to paint my vanity lilac (which is one of my favourite colours), and I have a poster of a lighthouse being swallowed up by a giant wave. Sami says that this picture makes her feel worried, but I love it. One day, I want to stand at the top of a lighthouse and feel the power of the wind whipping around me.

Hang on. There's a tap on my door . . .

Back again! It was Dad, asking how school's going and at the same time noticing the banana smooshed into my doona cover. Oops . . . it must have been from my schoolbag. I have a habit of emptying my bag on my bed after school.

I told him that school was going all right. But this year is off to a weird start. Normally, I really like the part where you get a new pencil case, a new set of gel pens and even a new USB. We all go off to Officeworks and we're allowed to choose whatever we like. Next year, in high school, I'll get a laptop like Annie, which will be pretty cool.

But this year is already losing its glimmer of hope. I've already lost some new pens. I haven't got my new highlighter pack back from Sami after I loaned it to her last week. And I can't find my compass set. I also accidentally ripped the back cover of my Social Science project book, and it's only the second week of school. Let's not even mention some of the boys in my class, the fact that Anh has hardly been able to come to school this year, and the incident of the uniform – which Mum keeps reminding me about . . .

'Did you return the uniform?' she asked at dinner. 'I tried to wash that smell out of it. I don't know how you put up with it, Alice. It stunk to high heaven of mothballs.'

It's the gift that keeps on giving, Mum.

Beside me, Annie sniggered. 'It was pretty gross,' Annie said. 'I could smell you coming down the hallway.'

I clenched my knife and fork a bit harder. 'I'll take it back this week. Good riddance,' I said. And then, determined to take control of the dinner conversation and change the subject from mothballs, I told them about Mrs Malouf's writing project this term, and how I didn't have a choice but that I got you, Greta, to write to. But Annie is *so* annoying and hardly listens to anything I say and started rolling her eyes, like my story was the most tiresome in the world.

I try to ignore Annie, I really do. She's only four years older than me but she's four thousand times more annoying than your average human being. She didn't even let me finish my story, but cut me off to tell her own.

'I'm already chatting to this cool climate-change activist from Canada on TikTok,' said Annie, matter-of-factly. 'You can just reach out to people, you know, Alice. Hit them up on socials. Email is soooo lame. Especially emails you don't send. What a crack-up!' Annie laughed overly hard; drawing looks from even my parents.

Ugh.

'It's part of my assignment, Annie,' I said, sarcastically. 'Mrs Malouf wouldn't understand TikTok.'

'Mrs Malouf probably has her own account.' Annie slipped her phone out of her pocket and started scrolling.

'No phones at the table!' Mum said, almost as an automatic reflex.

I smiled sweetly at Annie as she slipped her phone back into her pocket.

'I'd love to write to my hero,' said Mum, wistfully. 'Who would be your hero?' Mum looked at me.

'Well, I got *given* Greta Thunberg.'

'You know Greta won a million euros, don't you?' Annie interrupted.

Nope, I did not know that. A million euros, Greta? So – I need to research your show *and* your money. I'm going to look up the trailer of the documentary about you right now.

Best wishes,
Alice Boghosian

SAVE FILE TAB 11

Alice Boghosian

Class 6O – Library writing project

Tuesday 9 February 2021

Dear Greta,

You *donated* the entire million euros? You didn't keep even a hundred thousand for yourself? Or two thousand? Or even fifty little ones? That would have been so tempting. But the thing I'm beginning to learn about you is that you really mean everything you say. You don't do things by halves. You donated the entire amount towards saving the environment and climate change. I don't know if I could be as selfless as you – ever.

Sorry this is a short letter. Instead of writing this lesson, I've been doing some more reading about you. It's interesting putting together the pieces of your life. And it's weird to think we're only a few years apart in age. Mrs Malouf has let us use the iPads from the iPad trolley today, so I've chosen a spot on a beanbag tucked away behind the library shelves to sit on my iPad and research you. I'm guessing Mrs Malouf is okay with everything I've been writing because she's leaving me to it, whereas I can hear her having a serious talk to Jayden Tutai, who has apparently only written three sentences so far on this project. It probably reads like this:

- Dear James Tamou,
- I love you.
- What kind of footy boots do you wear?

Anyway, that's mean, but, come on, it's pretty funny . . .? 🤣

Chat soon,
Alice Boghosian

SAVE FILE TAB 12

Alice Boghosian

Class 6O – Library writing project

Wednesday 10 February 2021 (pm)

Dear Greta,

Mum is going through another one of her de-cluttering phases. Tonight, I found her wedged between her bedroom door and her wardrobe. There was stuff everywhere.

'Do I really need these gumboots, Alice?' She held aloft a pair of pink wellingtons that no adult should ever wear.

I shook my head. 'Gotta go,' I confirmed.

'Out the door,' Mum said, tossing the boots on to an even larger pile of clothes across the room.

'How's your Greta-writing going?' Mum asked.

'It's all right, but I found out something about her today . . .' I said.

Mum looked up. 'You okay?'

'Greta was really depressed for a while,' I said. 'So depressed that she didn't even want to talk.'

Mum put down a woolly scarf, and motioned for me to sit with her on the bed.

'Did it make *you* feel sad?'

I nodded. It did. It made me feel upset for you, Greta.

'She also has Asperger's, Mum,' I said. 'It means she's autistic. And she didn't eat for a long time – when she was stressed.'

'Autism is a spectrum,' Mum said, pulling me in for a hug. 'Which means it affects everyone who has it very differently. Greta has been pretty open about her own experience and having Asperger's.'

'How do you know about it?' I asked.

'I've been doing a bit of research on her, too,' said Mum. 'And I found out that Greta thinks it's her superpower. I think she's very strong to tell the world about herself. Asperger's is part of what makes her who she is, which is a very powerful and strong person.'

I feel a bit embarrassed now about all the

whinging I've done to you in my emails so far, Greta. The things I've told you about seem a bit silly – ridiculous nicknames and ignorant boys, and my annoying sister.

I just want to tell you that I'm here for you, if you ever decide you want to write back, or take a short break from activism or hear some interesting stories from a little place called Melwood in Sydney. You know how to get in touch.

Thanks for being so strong, for all of us.

Bye for now,
Alice

SAVE FILE TAB 13

Alice Boghosian

Class 6O - Library writing project

Thursday 11 February 2021

Dear Greta,

I finally watched the documentary on you last night, and the part where you decide to travel to the UN conference by sailboat is just intense! Did your dad drive you nuts for the whole trip? Were you scared of falling overboard and being eaten by sharks? (I would have been.)

It was a genius idea – to prove to people that you can travel without using planes – but I think you were super strong to actually do it. Even stronger that you stood up in front of the world's leaders to tell them that something urgently has to be done.

Were you scared of living on a boat? I am pretty sure I would be scared of not seeing land any more.

Were you sad to leave your mum, sister and dogs behind?

Anyway, it must have been really hard to do what you did, especially because you like routine. (Your dad said that was part of having Asperger's.) Annie ended up watching the documentary with me, and we've been talking about you ever since.

We haven't agreed on anything in a long time, but we both think you're amazing.

Best wishes,
Alice

SAVE FILE TAB 14

Alice Boghosian

Class 6O – Library writing project

Friday 12 February 2021

Dear Greta,

Do you think you would ever consider sailing a boat here? Like the one you went on when you voyaged across to New York? I think you would really like Australia, but, I have to admit, it's a really long way away from Sweden. Even a flight from here to Stockholm takes twenty-six hours without stopovers!

The thing about living in Sydney is that you pretty much have to get on a plane to go anywhere else in the world because we are so far away! And Australia is so big that it takes ages to get anywhere by car. There are so many places that I want to see that are literally on the other side of the world.

Here are some of the places I want to go: New York City, London, Jerusalem and Honolulu.

New York City: why wouldn't you? Everything great is there: Statue of Liberty, Empire State Building, Central Park . . . should I go on?

London: I want to see Buckingham Palace, and also the mounted guards that wear the special uniforms.

Jerusalem: because my nene was born there, and she said it's really amazing and talks about a place called the Old City all the time.

Honolulu: this needs no explanation. I love the beach.

Here are some of the places I've actually been: the Gold Coast, Bathurst, Wollongong and Gosford.

So, do you think that I should be getting a boat across the world rather than flying? That would mean my holidays would have to take weeks! (But that's okay, right?) Even a trip to New Zealand could take days to get there!

Flying across Australia from Sydney to Perth takes six hours, and it would be much longer by car. But cars are no good for the environment, either, are they? Hmm. 😕 The longest trip I've ever done in the car is two days to Queensland, when we went to the Gold Coast for a summer holiday a few years ago. Queensland is our neighbour state, but it still takes ages to get there. Looking at the map, Sweden seems kind of small (compared to Australia). How long does it take to get to your neighbour country Norway from Sweden?

This year, as long as there are no COVID outbreaks or hotspots, Year Six gets to go for a week to Hill End, Sofala and Canberra, for our senior excursion. Canberra is where our Parliament House is – I won't get any ideas. 😜 I can't wait for that trip. I really hope we get to go. So many of our excursions have been cancelled at the last minute because of COVID outbreaks. Lockdowns also really suck.

I haven't seen my nana and grandad in Victoria now for nearly a year, so we have to FaceTime them. It's not really the same, but we have got used to it. It's not the same as hugging Nana or playing cards with Grandad, or checking out what's new in their campervan.

Greta, please come to Australia for a visit! Maybe you could help us out with the environment and changing our governments' minds about what's important here. Because I've been looking into it, and no one at the top seems to be doing anything to save our wildlife or their habitats. Just take the Great Barrier Reef as an example.

Sami is nudging me now to pack up and turn the computer off.

Later, alligator,
Alice

SAVE FILE TAB 15

Alice Boghosian

Class 6O – Library writing project

Saturday 13 February 2021

Dear Greta,

Eight weeks. My life is going to be ruined for the next eight weeks . . .

Mum and Dad bailed Annie and me up for a Very Important Talk after dinner last night. I just wanted to Netflix. Annie wanted to go to her room and nerd it up. (Annie spends most of her time with computers and people on screens, whereas I choose to live my life in the real world. Usually in the privacy of my own bedroom.)

'Alice,' Dad said. 'We have something we want to tell you.'

It's important at this point to note that he said *tell,* not *ask.*

'You know how Nene hasn't been well,' began Mum, all seriousness and concern on her face.

'Yes, of course, I've been to visit her in the hospital, remember?' I said. Nene had a heart 'episode' a week ago, which had landed her in hospital.

'The good news is that Nene's coming out of hospital really soon,' said Dad, his face brightening. The stress of his mum being in hospital for the past few weeks was written all over Dad's face. He smoothed his hand over his forehead, probably trying to smooth the wrinkles that no longer go away. Poor Dad.

'That's good . . . right?' I said. I walked over to where he was sitting and got on the arm of the lounge chair and leaned into him. I looked over at Annie. She also looked worried.

No one is more independent than our Armenian grandmother. My other grandmother, Nana Irene, lives just outside Melbourne with Grandad Jim, and, before the state borders kept closing thanks to COVID, they'd come and go between New South Wales and Victoria all the time – they were always on the road. They'd stay with us when they came to Sydney (in their motorhome, which they'd park in the driveway) – to see us, and because Melwood is conveniently close to the freeway in and out of Sydney. It's extra-convenient for when they'd want to make a quick getaway. Nana's own grandmother was from Ukraine, and Grandad's parents were from Scotland. Last time Nana was here, she gave Mum her precious Ukrainian painted egg, which we put out at Easter. It's the only thing she has left from when her family lived in Ukraine.

But Nene (that's Armenian for *grandmother*) has always been around. She's always lived nearby. Nene lives in a granny flat in Albion Vale, which is just a few suburbs away from us. It's a tiny house behind the bigger house of a boisterous family, their dog and their bunnies. I'm not sure where *their* granny lives – I've never asked those kids, and we don't see them that much when we visit Nene.

Even though Nene lives so close, I only really see her at family birthdays and dinners. Nene doesn't own a car. She walks everywhere. She says she has everything she needs nearby – a grocer, a butcher and a set of shops. She goes to church most days. I honestly can't even imagine her being in bed for more than a day because she always seems to have so much stuff to do, whether it's cooking or visiting friends or talking to God.

So, anyway, that's when Dad told us that Nene was coming out of hospital this week. (Which is great.)

And then he told us she was coming here to live for a couple of months. (Also fine.)

'Yeah,' said Dad. He looked stressed.

'That's where you come in, Alice,' Mum said.

And it was somewhere between Dad using his serious voice and Mum using her persuasive voice that I somehow missed a key piece of information.

Annie's face turned into a smile. I could barely look at her. All I could think was: *Oh no, no, no, no, no, no*. Because that's when it finally hit me. When I could see where this was going. My bedroom, which is conveniently located between the lounge room and kitchen, with 'views' of the hallway, is the perfect grandparent relocation centre post-hospital.

So not fine.

'You're kidding,' I said.

Beside me, Annie stifled a laugh. Unsuccessfully.

'You're such a good granddaughter!' Annie teased. 'Giving up your own bedroom for your nene . . . You're going to win a humanitarian award.'

'Yeah, call me Greta Thunberg,' I deadpanned. Yes, Greta, I took your name in vain. Desperate times call for desperate measures.

'It's not like we're asking you to move out of home, Alice,' Mum said while I threw bundles of my clothes into washing baskets, all to be moved to the sunroom.

'The sunroom's tiny,' I said, dumping more stuff in random piles. 'It's practically on the street. I'm basically going to be a street kid. I'm going to dream about dumpster diving for food at the back of the IGA.'

Mum let out an exasperated sigh. 'You're so dramatic, Alice. When have we ever asked you to give up anything?'

I know I sound like a horrible kid, and I actually really love my grandmother, it's just that, *Year Six was supposed to be the best of my life.* But I'm not having the greatest start.

My life is over, Greta. Over before it even began. Why should it be *me* that gives up *my* room? I'm going to be sleeping on an airbed for the rest of my life – probably. Maybe I need to sit in protest at the front of my bedroom and block Nene from getting in and out. The world's press could come and interview me at my bedroom door, hearing my point of view about why grandparents shouldn't be able to come in and swoop on your stuff and take over your life. I could make a sign that says *No grandparents allowed.*

That's all for now,
Alice

SAVE FILE TAB 16

Alice Boghosian

Class 6O - Library writing project

Sunday 14 February 2021 (pm)

Dear Greta,

I am writing to you on Mum's iPad from an airbed stuffed into the sunroom where we usually keep *junk*. Oh, some of the junk is still in here, and I have to balance my iPad on my doona because *I have no desk or furniture.* It's also where Mum's upholstered furniture projects come to slowly die, with fabric peeled off everything, and springs and coils poking out of an old chair.

All my favourite things, like the tiny hippo statue that Anh gave to me and the new notebook and pen that Sami gave to me, are stuck back in my bedroom.

Look, I know you're too busy saving the world

and too famous to read all your emails, but I'm going to keep emailing you just in case you *are* reading and you could: a) give me good advice or b) help me do something about my crazy life that has been turned upside down or c) not respond, but I'll keep writing anyway because it seems to make me feel better.

This is something else I could potentially write to the UN about. Or maybe you could put in a word with the UN Secretary-General.

Anyway, I better put the iPad down now and get some sleep – if that's even possible on an airbed.

Alice

PS – Happy Valentine's Day! My inbox is empty, and I have received no cards from secret admirers (so far).

SAVE FILE TAB 17

Alice Boghosian

Class 6O – Library writing project

Monday 15 February 2021

Dear Greta,

I just got to school. Late. Luckily, library lesson is first thing, so I can tell you about my horrible Monday morning. Mrs Abdullah (our principal) told me off, and there are so many things that led to it that really aren't my fault.

It all started when I went into my bedroom to get my sports uniform and found my room had already been given the Queer Eye treatment, Middle Eastern granny style. Overnight, Mum and Dad had done some serious SWAT moves in my bedroom, fixing things and making it more 'liveable' for Nene, as well as filling it with Nene stuff. All *my* stuff from my bookshelf and vanity had gone. In its place were three glow-in-the-dark Jesuses and at least one Mary that had come from a trip to Vatican City undertaken in the 1980s before I was even born. My desk, which was perfect for reading my magazines, planning my life and drawing, was now covered with a gallery of old-school Armenians in a mixture of black-and-white pictures and grainy colour photos, all sitting on top of doilies. At least the doilies will protect my pink IKEA desk (I guess).

Hanging over it all I noticed the sombre, sepia picture of Nene's own parents, with their serious faces that have always creeped me out a bit; now, they are watching over everything in my room. (Make that, Nene's room.) Their eyes seemed to be looking especially at a photo of Nene and her husband (my grandfather that I never knew, my dad's dad), and another rounded gilt frame of Nene, with Annie on one side of her and me on the other when we were little. There was another, smaller, black-and-white picture of a girl that I couldn't help looking at – a girl who looked like a cross between Annie and me.

Honestly, Greta, Nene moves swiftly, and she's not even home from hospital yet! But that's when Annie caught me in the act of surveying my room.

'Love what you've done with the place,' she said from the doorway, a smirk on her face. 'So many icons, so little time!'

I am still fuming! Annie's computer fortress is still hers, but Nene has taken over not only my bedroom, but the *inside* of my cupboard, with a very neat row of black-and-grey knitted cardigan tops that must have been selected and transferred here by Mum. When I finally found my sports gear stashed in my vanity drawer, out of its usual place, I grabbed it and got out.

During brekkie, Mum and Dad fussed with the plans to pick up Nene from Westmead Hospital. And that's when it hit me that it was really happening. Nene would be living it up in my bedroom by the end of the day. And Annie's life would continue, business as usual. So. Unfair.

That's why I avoided Annie as we walked to the bus stop, deliberately walking behind her. She always wears her huge noise-cancelling headphones, anyway. She spends her life perfecting the art of ignoring me.

I waited a few minutes at the bus stop before making a big decision. I forged on towards the next stop, not wanting to wait for the bus here. I just couldn't bear to be around my perfect sister today. She has everything so easy!

Please don't let the bus come past while I'm between stops, I prayed as I walked. But, of course, thanks to my Alice luck, that's exactly what happened. I was still two blocks from the next bus stop when the 660 – that's the high school bus, Annie's bus – sailed past. That meant that my bus – the 650 – would be right behind it. So I started running.

I'm not the fastest runner in the world, and, suddenly, my backpack felt like lead and my shoes were like melted rubber sticking to the footpath. I was still a block away from the next stop when my bus whooshed by, and that's when everyone would have seen me running for the bus stop. That's also when they would have seen me take a spectacular dive into a hedge as I tripped on one of my shoelaces. For a minute, I lay there panting into the prickly bush, wondering if it was even worth going to school today.

I thought about going home and getting back in bed so that all of it could start over. But then I remembered – I have no bedroom, and my bed is filled with air. And so, I trudged to school with mounting fury. I was too scared to wag school and go to the shops. Ugh, Greta, I'm still so embarrassed about this morning, and then having to turn up to school with another dirty uniform and no late note.

No one looked more surprised to see me than Mrs Christodoulou at the front office when I trudged in at 9:20am – in another wrecked uniform.

'You're not having a good start to the year, Alice Boghosian, are you?' She looked at my uniform, with the new dirt smear across it. 'You look like you've been dragged through a hedge.'

'Funny you should say that,' I said.

'That's not the . . .' She looked at me questioningly. I could tell she was eyeing my uniform to make sure it wasn't the spare one she'd given me.

'It's not,' I said, pulling the neatly pressed, now clean, two-sizes-too-big uniform out from my backpack. It had somehow survived my face-plant incident with the hedge.

'I guess you know what to change into, then?' Mrs Christodoulou whispered across the front desk.

I nodded, reluctantly.

'You can use the staff toilet to change,' Mrs C said, gesturing for me to head deeper into the bowels of the front office.

That's when the principal, Mrs Abdullah, walked out of her office. She did not look happy. 'Hmmm, your sister never turned up looking like this,' she said, looking me up and down.

My heart sank a bit lower.

As I walked down the corridor that separated the photocopy room and admin office from the principal's and assistant principal's office, the eyes of a thousand past students in school photos haunted me. These included my perfect sister's school-captain-and-dux eyes watching my sorry state. Faded students with eighties mullets looked on, as did kids from the nineties with undercuts. They all watched me take the walk of shame. The kids from the noughties and the tens with pink and green hair ignored me, as per usual.

I happened to glance into the assistant principal's office and saw our year adviser, Cortez, sitting there. He looked at me quizzically before I walked off quickly to use the staff ladies' room.

Greta, I think it's fair to say you and I are opposites. For a start, you've probably never fallen into a hedge on the way to school. You probably have a lavish bedroom that you've turned into an office so that you can get back to your thousands of fans and run your foundation to save Planet Earth. You probably have advisers to help you with donating the million euros from the Gulbenkian Foundation. (Did you know that *Gulbenkian* is an Armenian name? That's right – we're everywhere.)

I know you said the world is on fire, but right now it feels like my *life* is.

Yours sincerely,
Alice

SAVE FILE TAB 18

Alice Boghosian

Class 6O - Library writing project

Monday 15 February 2021 (pm)

Dear Greta,

What's weirder than coming home to find your nene living in your room? Finding your nene in your favourite comfy outfit, lying in your bed, FaceTiming with her overseas friends.

There was some heated chatter going on, back and forth across the globe. Nene's small form was stretched out across my bed, her feet in slippers and neatly crossed at the ankles. Nene didn't sound frail. She didn't sound like someone who had just had open-heart surgery. She sounded vibrant and full of life, with a slightly scratchy voice.

I was definitely not expecting to see Nene in my favourite hoodie and sweatpants, lying on my bed, phone in hand, yakking away. What about all her cardigans? Hadn't she looked in her 'new' cupboard? Did she have to choose my favourite pair of fleecy trackies that have taken two years to wear in for maximum comfort? And why today? (I was still stuck in the gross second-hand uniform with the vague whiff of mothballs. ☹)

Nene's urgent chat sounded like an argument until someone erupted with laughter. I can't really understand Armenian. It all sounds vaguely familiar, but even Dad doesn't know very much of it (apart from swear words, which he told me he definitely knows). Anyway, I could get the gist of what was being said. Something hilarious was going down.

Dad once told us that Nene made him go to Saturday School to learn Armenian when he was a kid, but he stopped going as soon as the footy season started. Sami also used to go to Saturday School, but her language skills were/are perfect – I think it was a way for her family to meet other Persians in the community. Too bad she's now stuck with me – half Aussie, half Armenian – and Anh, who's Vietnamese-Aussie.

I listened some more, watching Nene laugh and chat with her friends. I hung around at the door until she started writing something on *my* favourite notepad with *my* favourite Smiggle pen on *my* nightstand. That's when I marched into my bedroom to reclaim my territory.

Except I was foiled. Even though she had her back to me, she seemed to sense me – a grandmother's 'sixth sense'.

'*Janik!* Come here and give me a kiss! *Inchpes es?*' Nene said, spreading her arms out, demanding a hug.

(Janik or *jan* means *darling*. It is used all the time for both men and women, as it's a total term of endearment. Armenians are not afraid to hug and kiss. And kiss again. Armenian men and women kiss each other not once, not twice but three times when they see each other. I'm sure they would get some time back in their day if they reduced the kisses to one or none. COVID has changed a lot of things in the world – I wonder if the virus will change the kissing?)

'*Lav yem*,' I replied. *I'm well.* That much Armenian I do know.

I wanted to be angry with Nene, but I couldn't escape the Nene Hug. For someone who'd just had heart surgery, Nene's grip was surprisingly strong. She pulled me down onto the bed (my bed) with her while staring into the screen in her hands. I was trapped, Greta.

'Well . . . say hello to Marie, Marie and Marie,' said Nene.

The split-screen on the iPad revealed four older faces, each in different parts of the world. When the three Maries saw me they went bananas, waving and warbling at me, as if I were a shiny new granddaughter toy. For a minute, I forgot that I was a guest in my own bedroom.

Let me get one thing straight: my grandmother's best friends are all named Marie. My nene (whose Armenian name is Vartouhi) became part of the Marie group when they all grew up together in the Old City of Jerusalem in Palestine. The four friends all left Jerusalem as refugees, but each chose a different country as their new home. One Marie went next door to Jordan, another chose America, the other chose Canada, and my nene came to

Australia, where she quickly changed her name to its English version, Rose. (I suppose the nickname Vart wasn't going to be . . . well, great. I've already told you how cruel nicknames can be here!)

Nene had only ten Palestinian pounds to her name when she boarded the UN ship that brought her to Australia. My grandfather (who I never got to meet) had just passed away. She told me once that she chose Australia because she couldn't bear the thought of Canadian deep-freeze winters. Imagine choosing a new life based on weather?

It's amazing that they are all still friends after all these years, despite getting on boats and sailing away to completely different countries. Would Anh, Sami and I still be friends if that happened to us?

'*Shat avoreh!* Pretty girl with beautiful hair,' said one of the Maries. I wasn't sure where exactly she was in the world, but I could see that this Marie was sitting by a pool overlooking a magnificent garden.

Nene pointed to the screen. 'This is Marie in Jordan,' Nene said. Then she pointed out Marie in Canada, and Marie in Los Angeles. 'You're growing up so fast, Alice!' Jordanian Marie said, squealing in delight.

I absent-mindedly patted down my frizzy hair, the bane of my life. But looking at these ladies, what was apparent was that our hair was similar – curly and full. In fact, even Nene's was similar, but hers was pure white.

'How is life in Sydney?' This time it was Marie in America. 'We are choking here in LA under a blanket of wildfire smoke.'

'That's awful, Aunty Marie.' I know *exactly* what she means. I ignored her first question and didn't say: *my grandmother pushed me out of my room and now lives a cooler life connecting with her friends on the internet than I do.*

'How is school?' said Marie in Canada.

I shrugged. I didn't really want to talk about it. I could feel Nene's eyes on my face.

'And your beautiful sister?' It was Jordanian Marie again.

'She's not home yet,' I said through clenched teeth, thanking my lucky stars that she hadn't seen me in Nene's headlock on my bed. 'What are you guys doing?' I asked, changing the subject.

'We're swapping recipes,' said Nene, pointing at my notepad, the one she'd been writing on when I came in. 'I couldn't remember the exact method for a dish, so I called the girls.'

'Then we got chatting . . .' said Marie in Los Angeles.

'About cooking?' I asked. 'Should you be cooking, Nene? You just got out of hospital . . .'

'Pah!' Nene waved my comment away. 'It's nothing.'

'We are talking about everything! Cooking is part of life,' said Canada Marie. 'And we are celebrating your grandmother's good health and return home!'

Not quite home.

The three of them smiled out of the screen. I knew that at some other time, another grandchild would be held hostage under similar FaceTime circumstances.

'Love you, girls, but I've got to go now and talk

to my granddaughter,' Nene said, before hitting the red button.

Nene put the phone down on the bedside table. I didn't move. It was actually kind of comfortable lying next to her like this. And her arm was still crooked around my shoulder. Being trapped by an Armenian grandmother is harder to escape from than a Bond villain.

'How are you feeling, Nene?' I asked, as she stroked my hair.

'I feel good, *jan*! Glad to be out of the boring hospital,' she said. 'Let the recovery begin!' She squeezed my hand. 'Thanks for the room. And these clothes. I'm never wearing anything else again!'

'Haha,' I said. 'The power of trackies . . .' By that point, I had somehow lost the will to tell her she should not have been rifling through my closet. I pulled myself away from the bed.

As I backed out of my own bedroom, I kept thinking about childhood friends, friends for life, across the world. I can only hope that I will still be talking with my friends when I'm old, too.

Wherever we all end up.

Anyway, maybe Mum feels sorry for me because she's letting me use the iPad all the time now, and I'm writing this from my new-not-new airbed . . .

Goodnight,
Alice

SAVE FILE TAB 19

Alice Boghosian

Class 6O – Library writing project

Wednesday 17 February 2021

Dear Greta,

It's so ironic that I've now been asked to join the Harmony Day working committee when I have virtually no harmony in my life right now. Harmony Day is a day when we celebrate all the cultures in our school. Almost everyone I know at school comes from somewhere else, sometimes more than one place. Even me, technically. I'm Australian, for sure. But I have so much going on – you only have to look at my surname! Everybody likes to take pride in where they come from, and Harmony Day celebrates that.

But before we get to that, I have to tell you what happened at school today. It seems there is no escape from home life or school life – what am I going to do?

It's hard to say no to Cortez, who has been our year adviser since we were in kindy. His classroom is disorganised, but it never stops him from finding whatever he needs. I'm not sure what he does exactly, but he always seems to be doing stuff. Last week, he was the MC at our swimming carnival, and he's also our cricket captain, public-speaking coach, peer-support guide and computer-room coordinator. This week, he has a new mission for Harmony Day, and he's managed to pull together the least harmonious group of kids possible to work on the project.

This inharmonious day began when Ms O'Rourke called out Jayden, Lance, Sami and me after lunch, and passed us a note.

We all looked at the note together.

Dear Ms O'Rourke,

Could you please send Alice, Samira, Jayden and Lance to the old computer room demountable at 2:00pm? Thanks – Ian Cortez

We all looked at each other. Something was definitely weird here. And I really didn't want to spend any more time with Jayden. A lesson each day in the library was already more than enough.

Appallingly, Sami seemed a bit excited.

'What do you think it's about?' she asked, as we walked in a pair behind Jayden and Lance.

I just shrugged. I had a bad feeling about all of this . . . But Sami seemed super-happy just to be out of class, and she chatted her excitement all the way across the other side of the school – over the quadrangle and through the empty playground, through the empty canteen area that always seems to smell like a day-old sausage roll – to the demountable where the old computer room is.

The old computer room always smells musty. 'Demountables' are classrooms that aren't really classrooms. They're like pretend buildings. They were built to be de-mounted – they are temporary classrooms, but most of the ones at my school have been there for *years.* I think every public school has them in my state. Do you have them in Sweden?

Cortez's demountable is where computer

equipment goes to die. (And possibly us, too, now that we've been assigned this project. But we didn't know that at the time . . .)

'Welcome, welcome!' Cortez said very brightly when we arrived. His excitement should have been our first warning sign.

The second should have been that the computer room looked like it had been hastily tidied – the kind you do when your parents arrive home in the driveway and you haven't done any of the chores that they left you to do. The blinds were up, and dust motes danced in the air. But the desks still overflowed with old computer equipment, dusty mice, ancient hard drive towers and old monitors. We use the library now for computer lessons, but when we first started school, we were mostly in here.

'Oh, man, I remember these from kindy,' Jayden said, looking at a boxy laptop on a desk.

'This is like . . . prison for computer nerds,' Sami muttered. She pushed the carcass of an old keyboard out of the way and sat on the edge of a desk.

'I dunno. I reckon I could still get these things to do something,' I said, thinking how much Annie would love the challenge of this computer cemetery. I chose to sit on a huge black case on the floor. There were several. They looked like coffins for the most useless of all the equipment.

I looked at Jayden and Lance and Sami. We all looked at each other warily, unsure of what to say or do next, in case we committed ourselves to something we didn't want to do.

'Found it!' said Cortez, holding up a remote and pointing it at the electronic whiteboard on the far wall. The screen blinked into life.

Melwood Public School: A Year of Innovation

'What are we doing here, sir?' Lance said, running a finger along one of the dusty desk surfaces.

'I need a team,' Cortez began.

A *team.* With these jokers? I looked across at the others. Even Jayden raised his eyebrows.

'I need help,' Cortez continued, 'if I'm being honest. We have a bit of a problem with Harmony Day this year.'

I noticed Lance mouth *no way* to Jayden. Panic was setting in for the boys, and for me. Sami, however, seemed oblivious. 'Isn't that coming up in a few weeks?' she asked.

'Are we gonna get out of class?' Lance asked.

Jayden perked up a bit at that. So did I, actually.

'Aren't we doing the Food Fair, same as usual?' I pondered. The Food Fair has always been a Year Six responsibility. I remember from when Annie did the Food Fair a couple of years ago that the teachers and parents did all the work and the kids got to take the credit. The way things should be, hahaha. 🤣 I remember Mum (who is technically Armenian now that she's married one and spent so much time with them) made Armenian kebabs for Annie's contribution!

'Because of all the new health rules and lockdowns blah blah blah, we can't do what we usually do.'

What I haven't said, Greta, is that the Harmony Day Food Fair is kind of a big deal. It makes the papers. It gets loads of visitors. Everyone gets yummy food from around the world. We celebrate being 'in harmony' with each other by getting together for the food and the games that go along with it. The thought that this year it might not happen made me kind of sad. It was bad enough that we might not be able to go on our Year Six excursion to Canberra . . . but the Food Fair is a part of our school life every year.

Cortez was probably sad, too. Usually, his whole family helps out on the Filipino buffet.

'So, what's going to happen?' I asked. My tummy lurched. Why couldn't things just stay the way they were?

'Not sure yet, exactly,' he said, cryptically.

Cortez shook his head and pointed to the row of big black cases. Including the huge one I was sitting on. '*That* is where you're going to start!'

The curious cases made of hard moulded plastic had stickers on them that read *STEM 4 SCHOOLS*. There was also a big white sticker on each case that had been scribbled on in different-coloured pen:

Cootamundra Public School

Chatswood High School

Hillston Central School

Maybe the kids in these schools had already suffered in the same way as we were about to suffer . . . Maybe they, too, had been forced to work with their mortal enemies by a cruel year adviser.

'Where's Hillston Central School?' I asked.

'Hillston, I guess, Alice,' said Jayden.

Haha. ☹

'What's a central school?' I wondered out loud.

'A school that has kindy to Year Twelve students in it,' Cortez said. 'They're usually in the country.'

Sami confirmed this by showing me her phone. The small red dot was in the middle of nowhere, in the middle of NSW. I have never been anywhere that remote.

'It takes nearly eight hours to drive there!' said Sami.

If you drove eight hours from your house in Sweden, Greta, where would you end up?

What had the other kids at this school been doing with the equipment? I had to admit, a small spark of interest flared up inside me.

'These boxes have done a lot of travelling,' Cortez agreed. 'And now they're here to make history in Melwood.'

Jayden didn't wait to ask if he could open up the boxes. He flipped open the latches on a couple of them, and Lance did the same.

But I didn't want to be outdone. I turned around and flipped open the latches on the box I was sitting on.

'What is this?' I asked.

'It's a 360 camera,' said Cortez. 'You four are now a team, a team of product testers. And what you're holding, Alice, is the *pièce de résistance*.'

I looked at the funny-looking camera, which looked more like a remote. Jayden and Lance were psyched. But Sami finally seemed to be seeing sense and cut me a look that said, *You mean we have to work with these guys?*

'Test out the equipment. See if you can film each other. And I don't just mean boys and girls – you have to do this *together*,' he said, firmly.

'This is all great,' said Sami, 'but what does it have to do with Harmony Day?'

'That's where *you* come in,' said Cortez. 'This year, Harmony Day will need to go virtual. You have a few days to put some ideas together – that's when I present your plan to the Executive Committee, including Mrs Abdullah – and you can use any or all of this equipment in your ideas. Once we get an idea approved, that's when you start the project for real. Now, time's a-ticking. Harmony Day is just over a month away.'

'Our plan?' I asked.

But Cortez was on a roll. 'Now, let's have a look at the equipment and see how it works,' he said.

Once we had unboxed all the equipment, we found we had two 360-degree cameras, four VR headsets and a charger backpack. Cortez showed us the basics for how each item worked. It seemed easy when he showed us, but more difficult when we tried to copy him.

'The school's your oyster, so why don't you kids start right now? Get thinking about how we could use all this for the Food Fair. Then get back to me.'

'Can we take this gear home?' asked Jayden.

Cortez nodded, so I grabbed a 360 camera, which seemed the easiest to use. The camera was small. How on earth were we going to use it to revolutionise something as full-on as a food fair – its smells, its tastes, the people . . .

Lance and Jayden whooped as they left the demountable. Sami flashed me a smile. Could we really be getting out of class to play with tech gear?

As we were leaving, Sami and I both saw it at the same time. Something poking out from behind the door. Anh's telerobot. It sat hunched over, her school jacket hung limply over its 'arms'. Today definitely wasn't an Anh Day.

But I'm excited, Greta. This could be our chance to make a stamp on Melwood Public School.

More next time,
Alice

SAVE FILE TAB 20

Alice Boghosian

Class 6O - Library writing project

Thursday 18 February 2021

Dear Greta,

If you had told me when school started that I'd be working on something as important as Harmony Day with my arch-nemesis Jayden Tutai and his henchman, Lance, I wouldn't have believed you. (Thank goodness Sami is also a part of the group!) Now, Ms O'Rourke has jumped on the band-wagon, putting us together in group work for regular class time, as well. What next? Bus buddies for our Canberra trip? (If it goes ahead . . .)

Today, Ms O'Rourke told us: 'I want to get to know you all,' which is code for *You're going to do another autobiography family-tree assignment.*

'If I do one more assignment on Iran and trying

to explain Persians, I'm going to die of boredom,' said Sami, and I stifled a laugh. I must admit, it took me a while to get my head around the difference. But Sami just explains it like this: Many people from Iran are Persian, and their country used to be part of an empire called Persia.

Last year, when we were in Year Five, we did a similar assignment, and it turned out there were over forty different countries and cultures we could all tie ourselves to. It's so complicated. Some people come from a country, or their families do, but they identify as something different. Lance and Jayden's families are both from New Zealand. Jayden is a Pacific Islander – his family actually comes from the Cook Islands – and Lance is *Māori*.

That's why Harmony Day is so important to us all. It's a chance to express who you are even if you are made up of lots of different parts and places. Even if you're still learning about them.

But our biggest problem still remains. If Harmony Day is all about food, and we're not allowed to cook – what's the point? And how can we help?

I fear the answer lies with the last person I feel like asking for help . . . My sister. But, Greta, I've been avoiding asking Annie for help like the plague.

'We're going to let the whole school down if we don't come up with a decent idea,' Lance said while we were meant to be working on our family trees. Suddenly, he was more serious than I'd ever seen him. 'I've *got* to do well this year. If I don't, Mum's going to send me to St Leo's . . .' Lance shuddered. 'I'm pretty sure she's already got me on the list.' He sounded almost hopeless. 'All of my brothers went there. It won't be any different for me.'

Everyone knows that the bad boys get sent to Leo's to be reformed. I'm not sure what happens there, but wearing a striped blazer, tie and shiny black shoes seems to be a part of the punishment.

'I'm going to St Kevin's,' said Sami.

I knew that, but realised something . . . 'There was a saint called *Kevin*?' I asked.

'He's a random Irish saint,' Sami said. 'I've been researching how to be a Catholic.'

'Don't you have to *be* Catholic to go there?' I asked.

Jayden and I laughed at the same time. I stopped immediately. So did he.

'I'm going to Whitlam High,' said Jayden.

My heart sank . . . Great. Just great. He's going to be following me around forever.

Bye for now,
Alice

SAVE FILE TAB 21

Alice Boghosian

Class 6O - Library writing project

Thursday 18 February 2021 (pm)

Dear Greta,

Me again. I'm home now, and I've started watching your videos for ideas. I'm hoping that something you say will spark my imagination to help me with at least one of the problems in my life right now.

BTW, your English is so good! Way better than my Swedish. ☺ Mum said it's because people in Sweden learn English as well as Swedish when they're kids. That's really useful. We did a term of Indonesian Bahasa last year, but I'm beginning to forget what I'd learned already. Mum said she learned French at school, and Dad did a bit of Italian, but neither of them can remember enough to have an actual conversation with a French or Italian person in real life.

Were you nervous speaking to those big groups of important people, in a language that isn't your first language? Maybe, if you have something to passionately argue about, it becomes easier . . . I get nervous sometimes when I have to speak in front of class. And that's in my own language! I'm not like Annie, who is really good at public speaking, and does debating just for *fun*. I mean, she's really good at arguing . . .

Annie says you can choose which languages to learn in high school, like Mandarin and Arabic. Saturday School still exists, too, but, like Dad, I don't think I want to go to school on the weekend. I used to play netball on the weekend, but it got interrupted this season because of COVID, which sucks, because I love playing netball. Normally, I play it every year. (Is netball a thing in Sweden?)

Nene's English is perfect, too, thanks to the school she went to in Jerusalem where she learned five languages from kindergarten – Armenian, English, Arabic, French and Italian. In a tiny school in the ancient Holy Land, kindergarten kids learned five languages. How do kids fit it all in their brains?

That's another thing – since Nene moved in and officially took over the kitchen, breakfast is not just Nutri-Grain any more. There's no escape from the Armenian MasterChef . . .

Nene cuts whole bowlfuls of tomatoes into tiny quarters every single day. In Nene's kitchen (and life), garlic is a lifestyle choice – not just an innocent flavour. Even at breakfast there are trays of salty, wrinkled black olives. And she dumps strips of Israeli pickles into a bowl from a can, with the juice and everything. There's usually a whole plate of garnishes – bright purple pickles, sliced onion and sprigs of mint. And bread. Did I mention the high piles of *kamaj*, the Lebanese thin bread? Next to it, labneh, hummus and a bowl of stringy haloumi that Nene pours boiling water over to soften.

It's not that I get a tummy ache or anything, it's just that I'm not used to eating like this for *breakfast.*

The strange thing is that Mum and Dad *love* it.

'Can't buy this in a cafe, Mum,' Dad keeps saying. He's looking happier these days than he has in a while. Mum can't get enough, either. Every morning, she hoes into a large bowl of hummus drizzled with olive oil.

Apparently, Annie and I used to love an Armenian breakfast when we were little. But neither of us remember this. However, we didn't argue when Mum said it in front of Nene.

That's another thing that happens now – Nene likes to watch us eat. Annie and I find it weird. We haven't said anything to each other, but I can tell she finds it weird, too. We're not allowed to eat breakfast standing up any more, either. Nene pulls out chairs for us and waits patiently until we lower our bums into them.

All the food Nene makes would be perfect for Harmony Day. But I'm still worried, Greta. How are we going to make Harmony Day work this year if no one can actually taste the food?

Goodnight, Greta.
Alice B.

SAVE FILE TAB 22

Alice Boghosian

Class 6O - Library writing project

Friday 19 February 2021 (pm)

Dear Greta,

Today was a good day. The 360 camera had everyone at school intrigued – my classmates, Ms O'Rourke. Now I'm getting the hang of how to use the camera, it feels pretty cool to be able to show it off to them. And Jayden, Lance and Sami seem to be enjoying it all, too!

I kept experimenting on my way home after school, and, by the time I was back, I'd begun to feel a bit like David Attenborough when he's deep in the Amazon jungle. I opened the front door and walked through it with the 360 camera switched on. So far, so boring.

'We are looking for the grandparent.' I spoke

in my best David Attenborough voice, under my breath. 'We might find her in the centre of the house, the kitchen.' (Or in a bedroom that's not her own . . .)

Sure enough, the smell of strong, bitter, Turkish coffee wafted through the hallway. I followed the smell and found Nene stirring a cup of the boiling black liquid on the stovetop in the kitchen.

'Nene, why can't you use the electric kettle like everyone else?' I asked, breaking my documentary narrative and dumping my backpack on the floor. 'And shouldn't you be resting? In your bedroom?' I tried to keep the edge out of my voice.

Nene was wearing her favourite outfit again from my wardrobe. I still hadn't managed to wrangle my favourite hoodie out of the washing.

'You're sure doing a good job of exactly the opposite of what the doctors said.' Annie's voice carried into the room, and I had to agree with it. For someone recovering from surgery, Nene would never be found snoozing on the couch, or in my bedroom. She was always busy doing *something*.

'Is that what I think it is?' said Annie, looking at the camera in my hand, which I realised was still filming. Annie suddenly looked extremely self-conscious, tucking her curls behind her ears. Her hair is shorter than mine, and can boing out to massive proportions if she's not careful. Interesting that her hair drives her mad . . . just like mine does me.

'What do you think it is?' I said.

'It's definitely a 360 camera,' said Annie. 'In fact, it's an OSMO Pocket . . .'

What a nerd.

'Did you say, camera?' Nene asked, absently fussing with her own hair now. 'Where?'

I waved the camera at Nene.

'Pfft. Doesn't look like a camera to me.'

I pressed the stop button and laid it on the counter.

'Where'd you get it?' Annie asked, with what seemed like genuine interest.

'Cortez got a box of stuff,' I said. 'It came from these other schools first. Some of them way out in the country . . .'

I looked at Annie as she picked up the camera to inspect it more closely. I couldn't just ask her for help with the whole project . . . could I?

'If only you knew how to use it,' Annie said, in her most annoying trying-to-sound-grown-up voice as she flounced out of the room.

That's it. I'm definitely not going to ask her for help. I don't need her help. I can do this myself.

Nene finished stirring her coffee and poured it out carefully from the small silver pot into a tiny Turkish coffee cup.

'Would you like one?' Nene was serious. She got a second cup off the shelf.

'I'm not allowed to drink coffee,' I said.

'Pfft,' she said. 'You can try it, if you like?' She pushed the sugar jar towards me. 'You might like it a little sweeter.'

I pulled the cup towards me, adding two heaped spoons of sugar into the dark liquid, stirring it. The smell was so intense, you could probably get a caffeine hit from just sniffing it.

'I got your dad to bring these from home,'

Nene said, tracing the outline of the bright artwork on each of the cups.

I remember them from her house and her tiny kitchen. There is matching pottery on her kitchen walls. They all come from the same place: a shop in the Armenian Quarter of Old Jerusalem, where a handful of families have been creating them for years. On the bottom of the cup is the word 'Jerusalem', in similar handwriting to Nene's – the way she seems to blend English letters with Armenian script, giving them a hard-edged fusion, and looking like an entirely new way of writing English.

'Is that *coffee*?' Alice asked, walking back into the kitchen. 'Mum's going to kill you.'

'You should try it,' I said, taking a grown-up sip of the bitter, black coffee. I tried not to grimace. Or gag. It was disgusting. I added a third teaspoon of sugar. I was determined to finish it, especially in front of Annie. But even four sugars couldn't help this drink.

'So, what's the camera for?' Annie pressed me.

'It's nothing. A Harmony Day thing.' I drank the remainder of the killer coffee in one fell swoop.

I felt it charging through my veins. The extra sugar was absolutely no help. 'You wouldn't understand,' I said over my shoulder while trying not to vomit.

Annie shrugged and headed to the fridge. Nene just looked at us both and shook her head. She sighed again. 'You two are very childish,' she said, and I knew she meant Annie and I and the silent war that was raging on. 'It's not good for my heart, you know.' She gave me a look. 'Harmony Day,' said Nene, drawling out the word *harmony.* Her meaning wasn't lost on me.

Anyway, the 360 photos from earlier are downloaded now, and, I have to admit, they're pretty good. For a start, it's almost like you're standing in the middle of the picture – like you're the most popular person at the party. (And, technically, you are – if you take the photo.)

A mush of scenes from Melwood, photos of food . . . I just might have the tingling of an idea.

Goodnight, and more soon . . .
Alice

SAVE FILE TAB 23

Alice Boghosian

Class 6O - Library writing project

Saturday 20 February 2021 (pm)

Dear Greta,

It's the weekend and it's raining, and I keep thinking about how you decided to just sit in the public square in Stockholm with the sign you made, rain or shine, because you were *so angry* about the world ignoring climate change. Were you nervous when people (adults) came up for a chat? In the documentary, some of the adults angrily told you to go back to school. You were so brave to even put up with that. They would have made *me* angry. And maybe a bit scared. I would have probably packed up and gone back to school.

I still can't believe you just went straight to the top, to the Swedish Parliament, with your own handmade sign and ended up starting a worldwide movement – as if it were no big deal – instead of going to school and putting up with your feelings, maybe with a little moan, like most people do. Your action on that first day continues to change the world! It gives us all hope.

Did you realise your handmade sign would become so famous and a symbol of protest? A symbol of strength and power to change people's minds and inspire so many kids around the world – just like me?

Were you hoping that some of the politicians might see you and decide to act on addressing climate change? Is that why you went straight to Parliament? I went to NSW Parliament for an excursion once, and it was a Very Serious Place. Some protests have been held there over the years – but never kids, I don't think?

When I started looking into your protests, I realised there have been all kinds of protests at our national Parliament House in Canberra, too, like the Aboriginal Tent Embassy, which is now a permanent protest site at our old Parliament

House. Over the years, the protests have been about different things but, at the heart of it, it's all about respecting First Nations peoples and their land. I really hope we can go to see the Tent Embassy if we do get to go to Canberra for our Year Six trip.

'Still putting people on islands, like the convicts,' Nene sighed, clucking her tongue looking at the miserable faces of one poor family still living on Christmas Island.

We're all sitting together in the lounge, and because Nene controls the TV these days, Mum lets me use the iPad more, so I'm writing to you while the news is on.

'If that had happened to me when I came to Australia, I might have been sent back home. And there was no place for me to go home to,' she says. 'There's probably no place for these people, either, in Sri Lanka.'

I think about what Nene said: that would mean no Mum meeting Dad, and no me (and no Annie). That would mean no home. Imagine coming across the world in search of a new home because your old home no longer exists – and then being sent back. The thought sends shivers up my spine.

I can't stop looking at the faces of the children on TV – the sisters aren't much younger than Annie and me. 'They don't even go to school?' I ask.

'We've become heartless,' Mum agrees with Nene. 'None of us would be here if immigrants and refugees were treated like this fifty years ago.'

So, everyone is from somewhere else, Greta. Even if you're born here. Unless you are a First Nations Australian. Is it the same in Sweden?

The next news item is about how California is basically on fire. And then about Greenland's polar ice shelves melting. They just showed pictures of icebergs floating away under pink-hued skies. Strangely, it's hard to imagine that something so beautiful is so terrifying. Actually, Greenland isn't that far away from Sweden, is it? Is it hotter than it used to be in Sweden? Are chunks of your country about to drift away, too? Our Australian summers are so much hotter these days. Even Mum tells me that.

'This is depressing,' Mum says. 'Not a single good news story.'

'That's enough!' Dad turns the TV on mute. 'It never gets any better! The bad news isn't just all over the world, it's here, too, in Melwood.'

We all just look at him. Dad never gets angry or upset with work, and so this must be Serious.

'What do you mean?' asks Mum.

Dad sighs and throws himself back in his armchair. 'The Council decided against the nature reserve.'

Dad is a scientist with Sydney Water. He is obsessed with clean water, healthy trees and the tree roots where everything starts. You'd really like him, Greta.

'That sucks, Dad,' I say. 'What about the ecosystem?'

Dad looks at me. Annie sniggers. It annoys me.

'What?' I defend myself, feeling my cheeks go a little bit pink. 'I'm allowed to be interested in the environment, aren't I?'

'So, the freeway exit is going in?' asks Annie.

Trust *her* to know everything.

Dad nods. 'It's going to be all concrete and land clearing and car emissions.' The more Dad speaks, the sadder he looks. 'We had the chance to really protect this area and preserve the birdlife. There's a species of wetland frog that's basically on its last legs. It's not found anywhere else in Sydney any more.'

Dad actually looks defeated; his shoulders are hunched. I look at Mum and Annie in alarm, and Annie raises her eyebrows.

Nene puts the remote down and looks squarely at Dad. 'You have to fight. You have to keep fighting. You are *Armenian*. We don't give up. If we gave up a hundred years ago and said "it's all too hard", Armenians wouldn't even be here. *We* wouldn't be here, together.'

Nene's parents had escaped the Armenian genocide, something that happened in the early 1900s, when Armenians were persecuted for being Christians. It's why Armenians feel such a strong connection with each other – such a sense of survival. And even though it happened a long time ago, even I still feel a connection to it, to Nene's parents, to the picture she has on her wall (my wall), and I imagine them living life in fear as refugees, having to run from their home country of Turkey and ending up in Palestine.

There have been so many sacrifices made for us. Maybe there aren't any grand family heirlooms, like those you see in movies or TV shows – things like old chests full of dresses and photos. No. The things that we have are Nene's few photos . . . and her recipes.

Her recipes . . . Greta, I have a tiny flicker of an idea for Harmony Day, and it's growing in my mind even as I write this. Watch this space . . .

Goodnight,
Alice

SAVE FILE TAB 24

Alice Boghosian

Class 6O – Library writing project

Sunday 21 February 2021

Dear Greta,

I've woken up to my heart beating so hard, and I swear I can smell smoke in the air. It's the bushfire dream. I had it again last night. It was just like Black Summer all over again. Hot, brown smoke filled the air, and the sky was constantly dark (like being in a dream). The air felt thick. Koalas with burnt paws were being rescued from the side of the road, just like what was shown on the news, and kangaroos were jumping away from the red ribbons of fire.

You were right, Greta. You had to do it. You had to start the conversation. But is it too late now to just talk about it? Can we get all the plastics out of the ocean? Can we save wildlife from all the bushfires around the world if we can't even save some frogs in Melwood? Does the Harmony Day Food Fair even matter? Can I help save refugees from their terrible situations around the world?

Sorry to be so dramatic today, Greta. But I can still see my dream, and Nene's big speech from last night is still on my mind.

Surely, there's more I can *do*.

Alice

SAVE FILE TAB 25

Alice Boghosian

Class 6O – Library writing project

Sunday 21 February 2021 (pm)

Dear Greta,

I spent the whole day stressing about it, but I finally put my life on the line to overcome the one hurdle in the way of my Harmony Day idea succeeding. Annie. I realised that I had to talk to her. Even worse, ask her for help.

'Don't touch anything,' Annie warned, when I entered her bedroom. 'Sit. On the bed.' She pointed at the one triangle of spare space. 'What is this all about?' she asked, sinking into her ergonomic chair and swinging around like they do on *Shark Tank* or *The Voice*.

Three computer monitors were lined up neatly across her desk. My desk is normally full of coloured pens and pencils, journals and magazines. I have no high-tech stuff apart from an old mouse (with a cord). But Annie has a place for everything – her cables are neatly wound up with ties, and her video conferencing headset that she got for Christmas last year hangs on a special hook. Most teenagers ask for money or clothes or . . . cool stuff. Not Annie. She even has a neatly stacked pile of folders on the bookshelf next to her desk. *Robotics Club, AR Working Group, Premier's Youth Advisory Committee.*

Greta, she's a Boardroom Teenager.

'I need help with Harmony Day,' I whispered.

'What was that?' Annie asked, cupping her ear like an old person. She really was trying to torture me by dragging it out. She was enjoying it way too much.

'I need help,' I said, a bit louder.

'Is this about Harmony Day?' she asked, her gaze steely and focused.

I nodded.

'I thought you didn't want me involved . . .' She swung back towards her monitors, fingers flying across the keyboard, tapping away at something she couldn't turn away from.

I swallowed hard. Looked like I had missed my chance. She was either going to help me or laugh at me. I couldn't handle either scenario. As much as I didn't want to ask her for help, she really is an ideas person . . .

'You obviously need help,' she said, and I let out a small sigh. For a second, neither of us said anything.

'Okay – so 360 cameras are pretty great. You can build whole worlds online with them.'

'You lost me at building whole worlds,' I said.

Annie's middle screen flashed up with an image of the Eiffel Tower, or what I could tell was the bottom of the Eiffel Tower.

'See this?' Annie said, excitedly. 'Three-sixty filming takes you *there* in 360 degrees.' Annie tweaked the mouse and, suddenly, the view moved upwards and we were looking right up through the middle of the Eiffel Tower.

'That's very cool,' I breathed. Then Annie switched from France, away from the City of

Light, and we were in Egypt, looking at a pyramid. I could almost see the ancient layers of dust and the grains of sand.

'See what's possible?' Annie said. 'Even with a basic 360 camera, you can take pretty amazing pictures. You even have the option to turn it into a 3D experience . . .'

'Hold up,' I said, still looking across the desert sands of Egypt. Slowly, my idea was taking shape in my mind. 'What if we took photos of *food* in 360 . . .' I said, looking fervently at Annie. Her face mirrored mine. She nodded. My mind was racing. 'Food in a kitchen, being cooked . . . or a barbecue . . . we could get everyone to take photos of their national dishes at home . . .'

'. . . in 360,' Annie finished, high-fiving me. 'Excellent idea, Alice,' she said.

Well, that went better than I expected, Greta!

Goodnight.
Alice

SAVE FILE TAB 26

Alice Boghosian

Class 6O – Library writing project

Monday 22 February 2021

Dear Greta,

My tummy has been flip-flopping all day.

At first, it was because I was nervous – now, it's because I'm excited.

This morning, I had to present my idea to the 'team' and Cortez. I didn't even have the chance to tell Sami about the idea first because it was her turn to run late for school today. Once I'd finished explaining my idea, there was silence. I honestly thought I'd messed up and come up with something silly. Then, Sami hugged me.

'You're a genius, Alice!' Sami said. 'I *can't* believe you didn't tell me before now!'

'Yeah,' said Jayden, smiling. He didn't quite call

me a genius, but I could tell that he liked the idea.

'We could get everyone to take a photo in their kitchen, or wherever they cook,' Lance said, wondering out loud.

'What do you mean?' I asked.

'Like a wedding or a christening or something like that,' he mumbled.

'Great idea,' I said. I loved how they were all already helping the idea to gain momentum!

'The hardest part will be organising everyone,' said Sami, going into Boss Mode. 'But I *think* I have an idea for how we could create a website for it . . .'

Cortez clapped his hands with glee. 'I *knew* you four would have this,' he said.

All morning, I could tell none of us could concentrate in class. Jayden, Lance, Sami and I kept stealing glances at each other. 10:01 came and went – that meant that Cortez was presenting the idea to the principal. It was very hard to concentrate on igneous, sedimentary and metamorphic rocks, which just seemed really boring compared to turning a festival of food into an online celebration.

When the bell rang for recess, the four us grabbed our bags and ran down to the demountable. Lance was first across the quadrangle – if Mrs Abdullah didn't like the idea, St Leo's would be looking more and more like Lance's future.

'GENIUS,' was all Cortez said. 'Your idea has been *accepted* by Mrs Abdullah and the school executive.'

'Woohoo!' I yelled.

The others just looked at me and burst into laughter. But I wasn't about to be embarrassed – I was so happy. This felt good! I realised this must be how Annie feels all the time!

'You're already really taking this idea in the right direction,' said Cortez. 'The technology angle is fantastic. You can always count on the Boghosians. You and Annie are so alike! Now, go and enjoy your recess,' he said.

Greta, Cortez's words have been in my head all afternoon. *You and Annie are so alike.* That makes me just a teeny bit happy. Emphasis on *teeny.*

Yours, in inspiration,
Alice

SAVE FILE TAB 27

Alice Boghosian

Class 6O - Library writing project

Tuesday 23 February 2021

Dear Greta,

'The Greeks gave us philosophy, the Arabs gave us mathematics and the Armenians gave us salad. If you ever end up eating with an Armenian family, expect lots of *salad!*' I was enjoying narrating my own cooking show earlier. I was the cook. Sami was the film director.

'. . . and cut!' Behind me, Sami was taking her role very seriously.

We've been 'researching' for our Harmony Day shoot at my place. We're investigating, plotting and planning our shoot with the 360 camera. Our team is still finding its way. The one thing we know for sure is that we are each going to do a test run at home with the 360 camera, to try it out. Lance and Sami are then going to build a website with Cortez's help – and, from there, we can build the 360 world for the whole of Year Six to contribute their favourite family dishes, for everyone to see. Jayden and I have to organise how we are going to share the cameras out, to give everyone in Year Six a go, and then we'll download and edit everyone's footage. I'm still not completely sure how we're going to get it all done in time, as our Harmony Day deadline is looming. The website's home page – Sami's brilliant idea – will be a world map with pins dropped in where each dish comes from.

'All this is pretty similar to Persian food,' Sami said, nosing around our kitchen some more. On cue, Nene shuffled into the kitchen and inspected the cutting board. I turned dramatically to Sami and her phone . . .

'Welcome back to *In the kitchen with Nene* – and, guess what . . . It's salad. AGAIN!'

Sami and I both collapsed in laughter. Nene just looked confused.

'I wonder what my *maman bozorg* is cooking

today,' Sami said, a little wistfully, then looked at her smart watch. 'It's probably the middle of the night in Tehran.'

Sami hasn't been able to speak to her grandmother for weeks now. The internet in Iran isn't great, and her grandmother's hearing problems mean that she can't hear that well on the phone. I have a feeling Sami misses her more than she lets on.

Nene started pulling out pots and pans, and Sami gravitated towards her, so I used the opportunity to change out of my school uniform.

'Getting changed!' I yelled down the hallway, which is what I do now as the sunroom has no door.

Sami thinks my staying in the sunroom is cool. I guess it's bigger than the bedroom in her apartment, but I miss my stuff. I'll be moving back to my own bedroom soon, and so I am not investing in the sunroom space at all. Because of that, there's just the air mattress, Mum's iPad and the naked-chair project that Mum started, which I use as a wardrobe, where I throw all my dirty clothes over the clean clothes and pretend the huge mound isn't there. I have almost blocked out the sound of the pigeons next door. Their warbling frequency is definitely getting lower.

By the time I'd changed out of my uniform, Sami and Nene were already cooking something up in the kitchen.

'I had no choice,' I heard Sami say when I walked in. I wondered what they'd been talking about as I fiddled with the 360 camera, checking it still had battery.

Sami is kind of the perfect partner for Nene in the kitchen. Sami has always known how to cook – whether it's making pizza or whipping up a chocolate milkshake for me after school (I mean, she has a milkshake *maker*). My cooking strengths are breakfast (ie, cereal in a bowl) and toast. Again, kind of ironic that I'm involved in a *cooking* project, don't you think?

I heard before I saw the tap running in the sink over some vegetables while Nene rummaged in the cupboard.

'Nene! You can't waste water like that!' After being a Child of Drought for years, it's second nature to not let water run down the drain. I turned the tap off. Greta, I'm a bit embarrassed about the fact that Nene wastes so much water. It's not the first time I'd noticed it . . .

'Aha!' said Nene, emerging from the depths of the messy pantry with a bag of cracked bulgur wheat held together by a clip. Bulgur wheat is brown – like couscous. It tastes nutty and feels rough on my tongue. On the counter were washed Lebanese cucumbers and tomatoes, and a huge bunch of parsley.

Nene gestured for Sami to come closer to help her. Nene and Samira genuinely like each other. I know my grandmother loves me, but she always has a special little job for Sami, or some nice words to say to her.

Somehow, this felt like the right time to shoot, so I switched the camera on.

'What are you making?' I asked, leaning in towards Nene.

'*We* are making *your* favourite,' she said.

Oh . . . I had been hoping to watch them cook, not help them cook!

'*Ashkily kofta*?' I said, hopefully, and Nene nodded, smiling. Out of all the dishes Nene makes, this one is my favourite. It's like an Armenian/Turkish version of chicken soup for the soul – except it's tomatoey and onion-y and full of floating kofta balls made from lamb mince and bulgur wheat.

Just then, Annie walked in the door and dumped her bag.

'Filming already?' she asked. I nodded. 'But you're not doing any cooking, Alice?' Which was true. I couldn't hold the camera *and* cook at the same time.

'Hang on, I have a surprise for you . . .' Annie said.

'Good or bad?' I looked at her, sceptically, stopping the filming.

Out of Annie's backpack came something familiar.

'Another camera?' I exclaimed. I was surprised and happy that Annie had got her hands on another camera. 'That will help us so much – can we borrow it to share out?'

Annie nodded. 'Thank Whitlam High Robotics Club,' she said. 'Now the school knows you're coming to join us next year, they considered you a student already. Just make sure it comes back in one piece,' she added in her more usual bossy tone. 'Plus, you need to be in the picture, Alice – time to get into the kitchen!' She playfully pushed me in, closer to the action. I was actually a bit excited to know that my high school was already eager to have me!

'Woohoo! That is amazing, Annie,' said Sami, as she moved across the breakfast bar to take a look at the new camera more closely. 'It's got all the right specs, Alice,' Sami said, sounding very professional. 'It looks just like ours!'

Sami took charge of the 360 camera this time, and Annie snapped away like a Hollywood film director using her phone camera and the other 360 camera, while Nene and I worked on rolling out the wet mixture of bulgur wheat and minced lamb.

'Where's the recipe?' Sami asked.

But Nene shook her head and pointed to it. 'This one's all in here. I've known how to make this *ashkily kofta* since I was a little girl,' she said. 'My own nene taught me.'

'Does it always turn out right?' I asked, watching her roll out the bulgur wheat and lamb mince into perfect, little round koftas. Annie leaned in for close-ups of me digging into the kofta mix, then rolling out the koftas. My koftas were odd-shaped and all different sizes. How does Nene get hers so neat?

Then it was time to wash up (this is why I avoid the kitchen) as the soup bubbled away on the stove.

'Why don't you have a bit now, girls, before your mum and dad get home?' Nene placed four shallow bowls on the table. With a ladle, she spooned out the red broth that had been simmering on the stovetop, and added three lamb koftas to each bowl, where they floated in the middle and cooked in the soup. Nene pinched out a little dried mint and sprinkled it on the top of our soups. The smell hit me, warm and comforting, something that had always been a part of Nene-ness. Annie and I have had this soup since we were little girls.

I watched Sami to see her reaction, and caught

Annie doing the same. At first, I could tell that she wasn't sure, but then her face broke into a smile.

'Yum,' she said.

'Double yum,' said Annie.

I leaned over and took my first spoonful. Yep, just as good as I remembered. Maybe this wasn't merely a screen test. Maybe this could be part of my Harmony Day contribution . . . I definitely had to get the recipe from Nene.

'This meal is from my mother's home region of Marash, in Turkey,' Nene said. 'The dish is a little bit Armenian, a little bit Turkish.'

'I thought you were from Jerusalem,' Sami said. 'Isn't that in Israel?'

'It's a bit confusing,' I explained. 'Nene was born in Palestine, but her parents come from Turkey.'

'And Jerusalem is in Israel now, but when Nene grew up there, it was in Palestine,' said Annie.

Nene shrugged, as if to say *it's complicated.* Which it totally is. I still get confused by it all.

'Oh,' said Sami. 'So, what country on the website's home page is your pin going on, Alice? Palestine? Israel? Turkey?' Sami looked at me.

It was a good question. The truth is, I'm Alice,

and I'm from Australia. But my family's history is a little bit complicated. And so is Sami's. And Anh's . . . Actually, I can't think of anyone I know whose background *isn't* complicated.

What about yours, Greta?

Gisher bari (goodnight),
Alice

PS – I'll send you the recipe when I get it. (You can make the koftas without lamb, obviously!)

SAVE FILE TAB 28

Alice Boghosian

Class 6O - Library writing project

Wednesday 24 February 2021

Dear Greta,

Fika.

Every language should have a single word for *taking a break and having a snack*. To my knowledge, I don't know if there is a more perfect word for doing two awesome things at the same time. Thank you, Google translator!

Fika. How do you pronounce it? Feeka? Or is it fikah?

'What?' Hannah's head just popped up over the desk. 'Were you talking to me?'

I now realise I've been talking to myself. 'Just thinking about this amazing Swedish word: fika,' I explain. 'It means taking a break and having a snack. At the same time. Isn't that cool? I just found it online.'

Hannah says there is a Korean word for it, too: *gansig*.

'Also a cool word,' I agree. '*Gansig* at recess?' I pronounce the word like she did – *gansik*.

Hannah looks surprised, but she nods. 'Yes, I will join you.'

'Good!'

My tummy just rumbled, and now I'm thinking about the popcorn in my bag. Actually, I've just realised, it's vegan, and so you'd approve of my *fika* food choice today, Greta.

'Would you ever want to be a vegan?' I ask Hannah.

'To save the environment or because of the way I feel about animals?' she asks me back.

I shrug. 'Greta Thunberg is a vegan,' I say. 'Do you think we all need to become vegans to save the world?'

Hannah looks a bit stumped.

As am I.

Do we all need to become vegan, Greta? I'm not

sure I can forego lamb koftas in my *ashkily kofta.* I also don't think my nene would allow it.

That's the bell. Time to go and have *fika.*

Hejdå,
Alice

SAVE FILE TAB 29

Alice Boghosian

Class 6O – Library writing project

Wednesday 24 February 2021

Dear Greta,

It's so hot today! The aircon in our classroom isn't very good, so Ms O'Rourke has brought us over to the library, which is why you have a second letter from me today. Mrs Malouf is a bit deflated, too, in the heat. Her sharp black bob isn't as bouncy as usual. Books waiting to be shelved have piled up on the library counter.

But the good news today is that Anh is here! It's been more than a week since she's been at school. She wheeled over to our group at recess. Greta, I tried not to look too shocked when I first saw her. Anh's face is thin, and her skin a bit pale. Sami looked at me in alarm, but I tried to keep smiling.

'What's been happening?' said Sami, before cringing at what she'd just said. We all knew *nothing* must have been happening for Anh.

'Oh, you know, flew to LA last weekend, hung with some celebs,' cracked Anh. I don't know how she keeps the jokes coming when she's stuck in her bed. Sami, Hannah and I crowded around the screen to make sure she could see all our faces at once.

'Guys, I'm okay,' she said. 'It looks worse than it is! Tell me all the goss, before we go into class and O'Rourke busts this party up.'

Sami drew breath. This was *her* area of updates for Anh.

'Thalia is going out with Joseph –'

'Ryan or Khaled?' interrupted Anh.

'Joseph Ryan,' Sami confirmed.

'That won't last,' said Anh.

'And Rhiannon is grounded for life because she sold her brother's bike on eBay for cash,' Sami continued. 'Alice invented a whole new amount of work for us, something she's cooking up with Cortez . . .'

'Hey, that's not fair –' I began, but Anh cut me off.

'Typical,' said Anh. 'Alice, you're always such a goody two-shoes.'

Which I'm not, Greta – I promise.

'Tell me some good news,' Anh said.

And that was recess, Greta. It's a good day because Anh is with us, *and* we have air-conditioning.

A coin just flew past me and landed on the floor. The boys are using it to play flick footy. Neither Mrs Malouf or Ms O'Rourke seem to care. I notice Sami is reading an old Judy Blume book. She must have lost interest in writing to her hero already. This is what happens when you hit Week Four of the new school year.

Looks like Hannah and I are the only ones working on our actual hero projects today.

'What sort of stuff are you asking Beyoncé about?' I ask her.

'About singing and church,' Hannah says. 'I'd love to sing, too . . .'

Interesting combo. I would have been asking Beyoncé about making videos, smashing car windscreens with a baseball bat and how rich she is. But singing is cool . . . if you're into that sort of thing.

Hannah doesn't say anything else. Sometimes, I just keep talking to keep the conversation going – she's so shy.

'I'm still writing to Greta Thunberg,' I continue. I don't let on that I write to you almost every day, and that I actually send you the emails – without even the hope of you writing back. It would sound silly if I said it out loud – no one else would understand . . .

'Is it your turn to take the camera home soon?' I ask. 'For the Food Fair? What are you going to make?'

'I'm not sure,' says Hannah, and she looks to me like she's slightly in pain. 'I eat the same thing every day.'

'Every day?' I'm thinking now, Greta, about how, since Nene moved in, we never eat the same thing twice, and how Annie and I fight every day for the leftovers that are in the small Tupperware containers, stacked up in the fridge. I feel bad for Hannah.

'Maybe Sami and I could come over and cook with you?' I suggest. But Hannah tucks her chin and bows into her neck, hair falling across her face. She doesn't say anything else, and so now we're both turned back to our computers, tapping away at the silence between us. I feel like I've said something to upset her, but now I don't know what to say.

Otherwise, Greta, our plans for the virtual Food Fair seem to be coming together. Cortez is happy, the principal is happy. I *should* be happy, but I will still have to work with Jayden on a lot of the project. I'm not looking forward to that at all.

Sami is working on designing the website with Lance. The idea is that when the viewer opens up our website, they see a world map under the title: Melwood Public School Virtual Harmony Day Food Fair. So instead of walking into our playground with all the food tents, people will virtually visit our kitchens from around Melwood (and the world). Hopefully, the 'magic' will happen when you click on a part of the world map, and the 'kitchen 360 shot' comes up of the Year Six person whose family and food comes from there, along with a recipe card of the food they're showcasing, and maybe some extra information that people can put together. The website can hold all sorts of info like flags, photos, music files, text boxes, along with the 360 photos that people send in.

Actually, I think we might need to make some notes for everyone, as a guide to help them with their entries.

Mrs Malouf has just dropped a batch of books about you, Greta, on my desk. It's a lot of books, but hopefully I'll get the chance to read them soon.

See ya,
Alice

SAVE FILE TAB 30

Alice Boghosian

Class 6O – Library writing project

Thursday 25 February 2021

Dear Greta,

Sami and I worked on a flyer to help Year Six with their Food Fair entries. We still need to run it past Jayden and Lance, but I'm sure they'll 'approve' it. This is what we came up with:

Attention Year Six!
This year, the Harmony Day Food Fair is going VIRTUAL. Harmony Day this year is on Sunday 21 March, and we will launch it the week beginning Monday 22 March as we are running a bit late!

Your organising committee is:

- Alice Boghosian
- Samira Hosseini

- Jayden Tutai
- Lance Henry

We are building a website, which will hold (virtual) food entries from all of you. Instead of bringing food to school this year, we want you to cook in your kitchen and take a photo while cooking using the 360 cameras that Jayden is organising.

All you have to do is:

- Take a photo in your kitchen using the 360 camera.
- Write a paragraph about where in the world your dish comes from, and why you like it.
- Other things you could include are: a recipe, a sample of the music that you cook to, photos of the country that it comes from, and anything else that is meaningful to you about eating this dish!

What do you think, Greta?

Alice

SAVE FILE TAB 31

Alice Boghosian

Class 6O – Library writing project

Friday 26 February 2021

Dear Greta,

Two hundred whales beached themselves on a remote part of Tasmania. No one understands why. They stayed in shallow waters for a day or so, with rescuers trying to push them out to sea, but then today they just threw themselves onto the beach until they died. Seeing their huge bodies on the sand, still breathing, then finally turning to carcasses has been almost too much to bear.

I can't imagine why they do it. I've been looking into it, because I can't stop thinking about it, and some scientists say that their sonar gets confused and they lose their sense of direction. But why do they all do it at once? Whales travel the same route year after year. They migrate up and down the same coasts in the same way, without even being taught. They just know. So they should know that the beach is the wrong direction, shouldn't they? Surely, in their pods, one of them sends a danger message or a *let's rethink this, guys.*

Maybe we're all a bit like that. When you're in a group that has made a decision, it can be hard to be the whale that says, 'No, I don't want to do that. I think we should head in this direction.' And then lead the pack to safer waters, not knowing if anyone's at your side.

Bye for now,
Alice

SAVE FILE TAB 32

Alice Boghosian

Class 6O - Library writing project

Saturday 27 February 2021

Dear Greta,

Harmony Day is becoming Headache Day.

I feel worried that we aren't getting the cameras in and out of everyone's kitchens quickly enough. Harmony Day is only a few weeks away, and we've hardly got anyone's footage in.

'Don't worry about it,' Jayden says, every time I bring up the problem. He doesn't want to deal with it, and I can't exactly force him to get more organised and stricter with getting the cameras back from people and passing them on to others.

I don't know why I'm getting so stressed about it when no one else is, but looking at the long list of people who still need to have their time with the cameras is making me very, very nervous.

Cortez raised his eyebrows at me when I was in stress mode yesterday. 'What's the problem?'

'We're running behind,' I said. 'I don't think we're going to get everyone's contribution in time.'

Jayden just laughed. Again. 'It's fine, sir. Everyone's working on it at home,' he said.

Cortez looked at me and then at Jayden . . . why didn't he just assume I was right? Jayden obviously isn't trustworthy . . .

'Well, lucky for you, I have good news,' Cortez said. And it was! Thankfully, he's managed to get us a bunch more cameras, which, along with Annie's extra one, will hopefully make the whole thing run more quickly.

Although now, I'm looking at this huge spreadsheet again of all the students in Year Six who *still* haven't done their filming yet, and I'm starting to panic once more. I just don't see how we're going to get it all done, even with the batch of new cameras . . .

Yours faithfully,
Alice

SAVE FILE TAB 33

Alice Boghosian

Class 6O – Library writing project

Monday 1 March 2021

Dear Greta,

Do you have a favourite book? Or a favourite hero from a book? Do you have much time to read any more, between conferences and media interviews?

It's been raining loads the past week, and so we've been hanging around the classroom at lunchtime, where Ms O'Rourke lets us lie on the reading rug and look at the books.

Hannah has kind of joined our group now, turning us from a three into a four. She's still very quiet, and I wish I could crack through her shyness *somehow* and get her to laugh along with all of our silly jokes. At lunchtime today, I tried to speak to her about books . . .

'This scared the crap out of me when I first read it,' I said. The cover of *The Witches* by Roald Dahl still has a hold on me. 'Have you read this?' I asked Hannah, but she shook her head and looked at Sami, who had her nose buried in a picture book for little kids.

'*Magic Beach*,' Sami said, quietly. 'This was the first book I read when I came to Australia. Beaches were literally all I knew about Australia before I got here.'

It's easy to forget that Sami only came here in Year One.

I sneaked a look at Hannah. She had picked out a good pile of books, ones that I would have chosen, too. Books have always been my friends. Sometimes, I wish I could read the Felix books all over again from the beginning. The first one, *Once*, I spy in Hannah's pile. Hopefully, books can be Hannah's friends, too, and I can re-live their stories through talking about them with her.

Later, alligator,
Alice

SAVE FILE TAB 34

Alice Boghosian

Class 6O – Library writing project

Tuesday 2 March 2021 (pm)

Dear Greta,

I'm writing from bed; today did not exactly go to plan.

I'm fuming. So, so, so angry. Worst of all, now, I'm embarrassed. And it all started with Jayden Tutai, who I hate more than anything else in the world (including depressing news about the environment, mass whale deaths and my grandmother living in my bedroom).

Not only has *Bogus* come back to haunt me, I've done something I'm not proud of, and hurt someone I love.

It all began when Hannah – who I thought knew me better – asked me the weirdest question in the world while we were in the canteen line. 'Is it true that you live in a nursing home?'

Even Anh sniggered on the screen next to us.

'Yeah, didn't you know?' I said, sarcastically. 'I have crocheted blankets on my bed, and I use a bedpan.'

Hannah looked alarmed. I honestly think she believed me, Greta.

'Do you work in the kitchen of an old people's home?' Montgomery Chu piped up in the line behind Hannah, holding out his phone.

What on earth? Where had that come from?

'Show me the phone,' I said, grabbing Monty's phone straight out of his hand and losing my place in the lunch line. Plenty of interested Year Fours and Fives watched on.

'What's going on?' Anh asked. I showed her before Sami and Hannah, as she must miss out on a bunch of stuff that happens because of the time it takes for her robot to move around.

It was a photo for the Food Fair that Annie had taken. It was one that I'd uploaded to the files for the Harmony Day website, on Cortez's computer.

The computer that Jayden and I were sharing for the project. It was a picture of me cooking with Nene from our 360 shoot at home. But it had been turned into a meme that said, 'Alice lives in a nursing home'.

'I'm going to *kill* him!' I said. There was only one person who would start something like this with me.

'No, you're not,' said Anh, through a mouthful of sandwich on the screen next to me. Anh was eating her lunch in bed today, and trying to calm me down. Although, she was actually laughing, but I really didn't think it was funny.

'Jayden is just being Jayden, Alice,' soothed Sami. 'I'm sure he didn't mean anything by it.'

That's Sami – always seeing the good in people.

Jayden wasn't far away. He, too, was in the canteen line, counting his coins. Lance just laughed in my face when I pushed into the line to confront Jayden.

'Why did you create that ridiculous meme, Jayden?' I said. Eye to eye with him, I realised he's just my height. 'I thought we were a team?' That word sounded really hollow now.

'It was just a joke, *Bogus*. Can't you take a joke?' Jayden looked around at his buddies, who all laughed, on cue.

'Yeah, it's so hilarious! I live with my grandmother. Really crazy stuff.'

'That's funny, Jayden,' Lance said, 'cos you live with the whole of Auckland at your place!'

I moved in then. I pointed my finger into Jayden's chest, and that's when he moved to push me back. I shrank back to avoid his hand, but I stumbled, losing my balance. And that's when the worst thing that could happen, happened . . .

Thud. Smash.

With a sickening thud, the canteen area went quiet. I stood there in horror. Jayden, too. We both stared at Anh's robot, which lay broken on the ground.

Sami and Hannah gently picked up the machine.

'Anh?' Lance asked. 'Are you there?' Lance gave me a worried look.

But there was no Anh. Just a cracked iPad screen and a busted telepresence robot.

I can't write any more, Greta.

Even writing this reminds me of how terrible a friend I am.

Alice

SAVE FILE TAB 35

Alice Boghosian

Class 6O – Library writing project

Wednesday 3 March 2021

Dear Greta,

The fact that I did something really, really foolish is making me sick to the pit of my stomach. The punishments and the detentions won't kill you, but the self-loathing will. I didn't want to write any more about what happened yesterday, but I'm forcing myself to. Call it self-punishment, if you like.

I can't get Mum's disappointment out of my head. And I feel doubly bad because she had to leave work early to come and deal with my foolishness.

'You're just so hot-headed, aren't you, Alice?' she said, as we took our seats in Mrs Abdullah's office.

'Do you think I'm going to get suspended?' I asked. 'Suspended' isn't a word that is even in the vocab of my family, but as I looked through the office window at Jayden and his dad, I thought for a fleeting moment that I, too, might be sent to St Leo's School for Terrible Boys. They might just make an exception for a Terrible Girl.

'Is everything all right at home, Mrs Boghosian?' asked Mrs Abdullah in a no-nonsense voice. 'Alice hasn't been herself lately.' She looked at me with laser focus. I prayed that Jayden couldn't hear any of this while sitting on the other side of the office door.

'The uniform at the beginning of term wasn't my fault. It was Jayden's,' I spat. 'And I missed the bus that time, and –'

Mum's look stopped me in my tracks. 'Now, Anh can't even attend school. That was the *one* thing she had left,' Mum said. Which was like a dagger to my heart. I blinked hard and fast to keep the tears at bay.

'The cost of the iPad repair will need to be split by both you and Jayden,' said Mrs Abdullah, gravely, looking at me again with disapproval. 'And, Alice, you'll need to go and see Anh, and explain why she can't come to school for the rest of this week. And, perhaps, next.'

I nodded. 'What about Jayden? It's his fault, too!' I looked at the back of his head, accusingly.

'Don't worry about Jayden,' Mum said. 'You think you have battles to fight, but this isn't one of them. Just avoid him and be the bigger person, Alice. Take the high road.'

Greta, the high road sucks. Do you ever find it hard?

'You need to sort this out with Jayden, Alice,' Mrs Abdullah said to me in a hard voice. 'It's getting to be a bit out of hand. I want you to sort it out with him before you find yourself in this office again. I understand the two of you are on the organising committee for Harmony Day, so that's the perfect opportunity for you to work together on your truce.'

At this point, I swear, she looked over to her wall where a framed photo of Annie winning a robotics competition, featured in the *Sydney Morning Herald*, took pride of place. I could almost see her polishing Annie's halo.

Alice

SAVE FILE TAB 36

Alice Boghosian

Class 6O – Library writing project

Thursday 4 March 2021 (pm)

Dear Greta,

Today was tough, but I got through it. Going to see Anh wasn't easy, but I'm glad I did it.

I was feeling nervous all day about apologising to Anh's parents, but I was also a bit scared of seeing Anh herself. It's almost like seeing the *current* Anh will take away from the *real* Anh. Real Anh is vibrant, has green streaks in her hair, is a fantastic dancer and an even better footballer. That's the way she stays in my mind, and I hate changing anything to do with that mental picture.

After getting home from school, I dropped my bag in the sunroom and left Mum a post-it note on the counter to let her know where I was and what time I'd be home. She doesn't get home sometimes until 5:30pm, and tonight she was working late to make up the time she'd had to take off the other day, thanks to me.

I zoomed in and out of the house before Nene could give me her 'disappointed' talk. I didn't stop to say *hello* or *goodbye.* Besides, she was busy chatting away to one of the Maries, with her iPhone propped up in the kitchen, in a fragrant cloud of simmering onions and sumac spice. Whatever she was cooking, I definitely didn't feel like eating.

I grabbed my bike (which, I must admit, I haven't used in ages), and cruised the long way to Anh's house, through Melwood Road shops and past the bargain basement store that was always closing down. Anh and I used to scour through the bins of that place, finding discount nail polishes with Arabic writing, clearly meant for a different country. There was the *pho* place we liked, too (*it's authentic*, Anh would always say), the kebab shop with the good chips and the empty dry cleaner's that closed down during COVID-19 because no one needed work shirts laundered any more.

Dragging the journey out as slowly as I could, I turned onto the main road and the entrance to the wetland reserve, where the freeway exit was going in. It's going to bring huge trucks through Melwood. So it will become even more loaded, with cars and trucks as people cut through to get onto the freeway.

Reluctantly, I turned onto Anh's street and pulled up outside her building. I felt sick, and lingered over locking my bike up in the foyer. I didn't even want to see Anh, but there I was. Her flat is on the top floor, and my feet dragged on every step.

At Anh's front door, I knocked and heard the happy feet of their pet Chihuahua, Muffin, scramble to the door, his little feet tippy-tapping as he waited in expectation. Voices from inside told me that someone was home. *Of course they were.* Anh doesn't go anywhere, except to the doctor's and the hospital.

'Alice, come in,' said Mrs Ha, smiling at me. Did I detect hatred towards me? Greta, there was not a sign. She hugged me at the front door, just like she always does.

'Anh's resting now,' she said, looking at me with eyes full of concern. I felt terrible in that moment and just wanted to melt into the floor. Instead of looking angry, she looked worried. And, the way she was looking at me, I realised – she was worried for *me*.

But, Greta, I was sick inside. Was Anh avoiding me? Was our friendship over? Would she ever forgive me?

'I'm really sorry, Mrs Ha,' I mumbled, not meeting her eyes. She ushered me into her kitchen, where she put a cold glass of water in front of me.

'Alice, don't be silly. We'll work it out.'

My eyes were everywhere except on hers. 'It was a horrible accident,' I said, my cheeks on fire. All I could think was: why are you so *foolish*, Alice? Why couldn't you just let Jayden's joke go?

'Is Anh mad at me?'

Mrs Ha clicked her tongue. 'Don't be silly, Alice,' she said. 'Anh thought it was funny. To be honest, using that machine makes her tired sometimes. She's probably going to take a break while they fix the robot over the next few weeks.'

The next few weeks?

'But she usually comes to school at least once a week . . .' I said. The *few weeks* hung in the air between us, strung out like a tightrope.

'Her doctor is making some changes to her treatment,' Mrs Ha explained. She always looked the same, no matter how tough the news got. 'Anh's going to be more tired than usual. She wants to catch up on her shows and her comics.'

Mrs Ha moved around her tiny, spotless kitchen, wiping at imaginary spots. Not a single thing was out of place.

So much was whirring through my mind . . . what did all this mean for Sami and me (and Hannah) and our friendship circle? And, how was Anh going to take part in the Food Fair?

'Do you think she'd be up for a project?' I asked.

Mrs Ha raised her eyebrows in question. 'She's going to be tired, Alice,' she explained gently to me again.

Okay – I got the message this time.

'Tell Anh I said hi – and sorry,' I said. 'Thanks for the water.'

Cycling home seemed way harder than going there. And I swear my back tyre's flat.

When I finally walked back in the door at home, I heard Mum's voice. 'Is that you, Alice?'

And when I entered the kitchen, Mum's face was thunder.

'Didn't you think to tell Nene you went out?' Mum was enraged, the vein on her temple popping out. 'You haven't answered your phone. Plus, you know you're grounded. Do you *only* ever think of yourself?'

No! I've got a million things on my mind! I'm trying to fix things! Everything is going wrong . . . I felt like shouting it out loud, but I didn't.

Nene was grilling lamb chops in the pan. She violently squeezed lemon over the meat. It sizzled like a demon. Clouds of smoke choked the kitchen, but she didn't seem to notice. She moved to the cutting board, hell-bent on slicing up vegetables for yet another salad.

'You chop,' she said, but wouldn't meet my eye. So, I wearily walked round to stand next to her, and sliced and diced my way through my

Mediterranean diet punishment. Annie's eyeballs flew between me, Nene and Mum, like someone watching a juicy, gossipy tennis match.

So. Much. Salad. I never want to see another Lebanese cucumber again. I'm going to have to chop my way out of this mess. While working out how I can help Anh to contribute to the Food Fair project. While working out how I don't kill Jayden.

More soon,
Alice

SAVE FILE TAB 37

Alice Boghosian

Class 6O – Library writing project

Friday 5 March 2021 (pm)

Dear Greta,

Mum is still giving me the cold shoulder. Dad keeps sighing to remind me how unimpressed with me he is. Annie is walking a fine tightrope between sympathy and being a jerk (not hard for her). This punishment feels like it's already gone on forever . . .

Worse than being grounded, worse than wondering where I'm going to get pocket money from to pay Mum and Dad back for Anh's new iPad, is getting the silent treatment. Both Mum and Dad are excellent at it. They could run master classes in it. I can see the ad now:

Learn how to be civil to your children while you

allow disappointment to seep from your parental pores! The Boghosians will show you how . . .

I'm only a day in to my punishment, and I'm sick of the kitchen, I'm sick of the sunroom. The kitchen is in the middle of the house, and the sunroom leads on to it, so I can't really avoid anyone. I can't really leave its four walls.

I don't feel like cooking and 'hanging out' with Nene. I don't feel like doing anything. I keep going to check my phone to see if I have a message from Sami or Anh, but Mum and Dad have confiscated it as part of my punishment. My parents seem to have forgotten about the iPad, so at least I can still write to you, which (whether you're reading my emails or not) somehow makes me feel a smidge better about myself while I'm grounded for life.

Otherwise, all I feel like doing is reading. I've pulled out the pile of books about you that Mrs Malouf gave me. I'll try and channel all your good energy.

Yours,
Alice

SAVE FILE TAB 38

Alice Boghosian

Class 6O – Library writing project

Saturday 6 March 2021

Dear Greta,

Last night, after I'd sent the email to you, Dad popped by the sunroom. He came to say goodnight, and ended up telling me so many stories that kind of link *him* and *me* to you. Isn't that nuts?

I had just picked up an old-fashioned book with a dust jacket on, from that pile I said Mrs Malouf had given me, and I was propped up on a pillow on the airbed.

'Whatcha reading?' Dad asked.

Was this a truce?

'Mrs Malouf's reading pile,' I said, pointing at her Greta Thunberg Library Collection, fanned out across my doona.

'*I* had that book, back in the day,' Dad said, plucking the book out of my hands. He lowered himself onto the airbed, causing seismic shockwaves. When the wobble came to a stop, Dad confirmed: 'Yep, the very one.' It was called *Saving the Whales*. 'God, this bed is uncomfortable, Alice,' Dad said, almost rolling off.

'Tell me about it.'

He shifted, eventually finding a comfortable position that was half on the airbed and half on the floor, while leaning onto the pile of pillows that I create for myself every night to read.

Dad opened the front cover to reveal a bookplate that read: *This book belongs to Jean Malouf.* There was also a sticker that said: *Greenpeace. Save the Whales*.

'What's Greenpeace, Dad?'

'Only the most important organisation I've ever belonged to,' Dad said.

'I thought that was Wests Tigers?'

Dad paused. 'Not even close,' he said.

Talk about Earth-shattering information, Greta!

'Greenpeace is an organisation dedicated to saving the environment and, in particular, the oceans,' Dad said. 'When I was growing up, it was a radical group . . . a bit like the Extinction Rebellion movement, which is around now. This was a member's sticker,' Dad said, pointing to the *Save the Whales* sticker. 'Looks like your librarian was one, too. You'd send away and get the newsletters and stickers.'

'Newsletter and stickers?' I said. 'Were you five years old?'

'If you can believe it, I was your age. It was exciting to get something in the post every month. You'd get a package of information, and stickers just like this one.'

I tried to imagine teenage Dad, eagerly waiting by the mailbox. I could tell he was lost in dreamland, remembering his parcels of mail from Greenpeace.

'They'd tell you what the latest missions were, and how your contributions helped.'

'Missions? Contributions?' It sounded serious, Greta.

'When I was your age, whales were being killed left, right and centre by some countries,' he said, sadly. 'For things like cosmetics. We thought whales would be wiped out by the time you and Annie and the next generation came along. Can you imagine a world without whales? Greenpeace went on missions, particularly in the South Pacific, to try and protect whales and the whole environment, really.'

Dad paused, deep in thought, and carried on flicking through the book.

'They called it "scientific research",' he continued, frowning. 'That's how they got away with it, some of those countries. Why would you want to kill such beautiful animals? That's why I got into science. To save whales. But I got side-tracked studying aquatic ecology.'

Dad sounded so sad.

'It's kind of related, Dad,' I said. 'You're still saving the environment. It's still to do with water.' I wanted to make him feel better, Greta. I could tell this old book was taking him back somewhere.

'Sometimes,' Dad said. 'Doesn't always feel

like we're winning, though. Those Green and Golden Bell Frogs we have living in the designated freeway zone may not make it . . . we can't seem to convince Mayor Pennyworth to keep to her original decision – to save the wetlands. We've worked so hard to preserve them, too . . .'

'And if I had my phone . . . I'd be able to look up what the Green and Golden Bell Frog looks like,' I grumbled.

Dad continued leafing through the book, and that's when the old newspaper clippings fell out. *French Nuke Tests Menace Pacific Lives* cried one article. *Rainbow Warrior on Important Mission* said another. The dates were old.

'Ah,' said Dad. 'The *Rainbow Warrior*.'

'The Rainbow what?'

'It was a ship – a protest ship. The French government blew it up. In New Zealand,' he said, shaking his head.

My head was spinning. This saving the world business sounded dangerous. Saving whales and tiny frogs and protecting the environment shouldn't be this scary!

'Nana Irene was absolutely outraged,' Dad said. 'It was a ship trying to stop nuclear testing in French Polynesia . . . they were trying to stop the French from testing nuclear weapons.'

Dad pulled out his phone and did a quick search, pulling up a series of chilling photos of a nuclear bomb blast, its mushroom cloud exploding and growing and spreading. The caption read *Test at Mururoa.*

'Hard to believe, isn't it? The beautiful Mururoa Atoll as a testing ground. The nuclear fallout killing everything in its path. They did so many tests that they killed that whole ecosystem, that whole environment . . . That's why the protest movement and the *Rainbow Warrior* were so important.'

'Did they stop the testing? What about the people that lived there?' I asked. I was starting to feel physically sick about it all.

'People got sick . . . France stopped for a little while,' Dad said. 'But they went back to their "tests", even after they blew up the *Rainbow Warrior*.'

I sifted through some of the old articles, finding a clipping of an article with a clear photo. It was

Mrs Malouf. She was holding a placard saying *No Nukes in the Pacific.*

'I think Mrs Malouf was an activist, back in the day.' I pointed to Mrs Malouf, her hair long and parted in the middle. Instead of her brooches, the vest she wore was covered in badges and pins.

'Just like your mate, Greta Thunberg,' Dad said. 'She's a very brave young woman. She stands up for what she believes in. I admire her greatly. I bet Mrs Malouf does, too. Perhaps it was no coincidence that you ended up getting Greta to write to,' Dad said, rolling himself up off the floor. 'Time for bed now, Alice. Night.'

'Night, Dad.'

I spent so long looking at the photo of a young Mrs Malouf holding her *No Nukes in the Pacific* sign in the old newspaper, that I dreamt about it all last night.

And when I woke up, I knew what her hand-made sign reminded me of . . .

It reminded me of *your* protest sign, Greta.

Bye for now,
Alice

SAVE FILE TAB 39

Alice Boghosian

Class 6O - Library writing project

Sunday 7 March 2021

Dear Greta,

I've been doing some research. And guess what I discovered? That Greenpeace is still going! It's an organisation that's all about saving the environment, endangered animals and protecting the world against climate change (though I'm sure you know all this).

I also looked up the Green and Golden Bell Frog that Dad's worried about. They can be found in Sydney's basin (aka Melwood) – they have a white belly and a green back with gold patches. They lay their eggs in the water, and it can take three to eleven months for them to turn into frogs. They grow to up to 8.5cm and they are *endangered*.

If they put the freeway in, there's a very good chance it will wipe out the whole colony in Melwood Wetlands. Dad said the scientists have been working really hard to build the numbers up. Why would you allow people to spend so much time trying to save the frogs only to then wipe out their habitat? That just seems so silly. I mean, if people want to get on the freeway, why don't they just drive a bit further through Melwood and get on the *next* entrance to the freeway. One that's already built?

I'm so angry about this, Greta!

Bye,
Alice

SAVE FILE TAB 40

Alice Boghosian

Class 6O – Library writing project

Sunday 7 March 2021 (pm)

Dear Greta,

Today, Nene had surprises in store for Annie and me. But Nene's surprises aren't always the ones you want. And this particular surprise happened to coincide with when it was my turn to have the 360 camera. Nene had already planned which recipe we were going to cook. And I'd planned how we were going to film it. What I hadn't factored in was receiving a gift from Nene that would mean I didn't really want to be *in* the shot . . .

'I got you both a present today.' Nene smiled at Annie and I mysteriously. I was secretly hoping for some new tracksuits, now that she's decided she owns mine . . .

'Hopefully, it was online shopping, Nene,' said Annie. We all know that online shopping makes Nene grumpy.

'Don't be silly. My friend Sylvia from around the corner brought them round for me.'

Sylvia was another Armenian nene, who lived locally. Nene slid two flat parcels to us across the kitchen counter.

I unfolded mine first. It was a pink apron with daisies. I reluctantly draped it over my head, tying it around my waist and bringing the strings around to the front like the contestants do on *MasterChef*. Nene looked so happy. I was just hoping that she didn't make me wear this for my Food Fair contribution picture.

Annie tore into her package, revealing an apron with big sprays of pink and mauve hydrangeas. Given that Annie wears black, black and exclusively more black, mixed in with the occasional Minecraft T-shirt, it couldn't have been a worse choice. You should have seen Annie's face!

Nene clapped her hands joyously. '*This* is what we've been missing,' she exclaimed. '*Now*, we cook!'

And she magically pulled out a bowl of minced meat mixed with onions and herbs.

Stuffing dolma seems like an art form. There are a hundred ways to stuff a vegetable with meat. I had a pen and paper ready to write down the steps as we went so that I could capture how to re-make it if I ever want to, and if other families like the recipe online and want to try it themselves.

'This online shopping business is no good,' Nene said. 'You can't choose your own vegetables. You get sickly, weak, no-good zucchinis,' she said, looking at the range of zucchinis on the board. They ranged in size from the weaklings to the mighty. To me, they all looked like the pathetic vegetable that is zucchini.

'I wish we had a *MasterChef* pantry,' I said, wistfully. The pantry dash used to be Annie's and my favourite part of the show. When the show sends stressed-out contestants with no idea what to cook into a pantry full of stuff. It was amazing what they'd emerge with. Under pressure, they'd sometimes choose terrible combinations, like chocolate, anchovies and leeks.

'I hope this meat mixture makes the zucchini taste disappear,' I whispered to Annie. I'm not the biggest fan of zucchini, but if it's stuffed with meat, onion and rice then it's kind of bearable . . . and if you also add heaps and heaps of Greek yoghurt . . . *Then*, it's delicious.

'I heard that,' said Nene, and Annie and I giggled.

But wearing an apron didn't make me a masterchef . . . I just couldn't keep the mixture together. Nene made it look so easy. Annie's looked as terrible as mine. Her stuffing was a big blob, and mine kept falling apart.

'Looking good,' said Nene, but I didn't really believe her. My dolma ended up overstuffed and fat, with mixture falling out. Nene's was neat and perfect with the lids of the zucchinis looking like little hats for vegetables. She seemed so happy in that moment in our kitchen, watching us struggle to make something she'd made her whole life.

Once the dolma had gone into the oven, I tried to capture on camera everything we had done for the recipe, with all the different ingredients.

Nene will have to check it out later to make sure I didn't miss anything.

Annie and I then hung around in the kitchen and tried to write down the recipe using the notes I'd made (with Annie helpfully pointing out every step I'd missed). The smell from the oven got better and better, and, guess what? They were delicious. I didn't even notice the taste of zucchini.

Bye for now,
Alice

SAVE FILE TAB 41

Alice Boghosian

Class 6O - Library writing project

Monday 8 March 2021

Dear Greta,

Public speaking isn't my favourite thing, and so I've been trying not to think about the presentation that Ms O'Rourke asked me to give to our class on the Food Fair project. Partly, it's a chance to describe what we're doing, but it's also a way to hurry people up to get their entries in and then pass the 360 cameras around so that everyone can contribute. Only half of Year Six (and half of 6O) have done theirs so far, and the deadline is getting closer. We have just two weeks! Eek! 😱

Jayden hasn't been saying much to me since The Whole Incident That Blew Out of Proportion. I took it as a good sign, though, that before school he offered to help load up my pictures so we could show them to the class. He was very nice to me, and didn't even laugh at mine and Annie's pinker-than-pink aprons in the picture that got uploaded in my file. Best of all, Sami and Lance's website that they've been designing with Cortez looks amazing. The virtual world map with all the dropped pins looks better than I ever imagined, and really makes you realise where all the different foods – and families – come from.

It's been hard to choose exactly where my pin for the dolma should go. Nene comes from Jerusalem, but not when it was in Israel, which is where it is now on the world map. And the recipe got passed down from her parents' families, who actually came from Turkey. So, I've decided to opt for both pins, and I'm planning on explaining why in my recipe board, which I still need to finish and upload.

Jayden's best behaviour continued when it came time for the class presentation. I spent all of recess stressing about it, and then I kind of blanked when Ms O'Rourke called me up to the front of the room. But Jayden stepped in and started things going . . .

'These are some photos that Alice took last night,' Jayden said, prompting me into action. He flashed up on the smartboard the 360 picture of my kitchen, with me and Nene and the dolma action, and everyone giggled. But I don't think they were laughing at *me* (it was the aprons, I'm sure). But once I started telling everyone about the whole project, it got a lot easier.

'My sister took this so that I could be in the picture with my nene,' I said. I could see my kitchen through everyone's eyes. The busy kitchen, the fridge with all the takeaway menus tacked onto it, the apricot-pink counters and cupboards that Mum and Dad are always planning on changing. And, in the middle of it all, my grandmother, Nene, with her hands in the mixing bowl with the dolma mixture.

'What if you don't have a big sister?' said Hannah. It was the first time I'd ever heard her say anything out loud in class.

'It doesn't have to be a sister,' I said. I guess

not every kid in my class has a brother or sister. 'It could be a . . . friend?'

Hannah looked embarrassed. I think I said the wrong thing.

'That's my nene,' I said. 'She's living with us right now. She had a heart attack a month ago, so she came to live with us while she gets better.' I was oversharing out of nerves, but, at the same time, I was trying to defend my reputation. I shot a look at Jayden, who went red.

'You can add recipes, too,' I said. 'I'm going to add some Armenian music that my nene is always listening to, and I was thinking of interviewing my Armenian grandmother because the story behind this recipe is interesting. She used to make it with *her* grandmother, so I'll write about that,' I said. 'We'll be loading up the recipes and all the other things that make up your recipe, too, so make sure you include those extra details in the email along with your 360 picture.'

'Well done, Alice,' said Ms O'Rourke.

I took a deep breath. I'd done it. And it had gone well. I think . . . Do you get nervous when you address big crowds, Greta? I know my classroom doesn't compare to the UN conference, but did you find it difficult to talk to your class when you were at school?

'Now, Lance, I believe you have a bit to show us as well?' Ms O'Rourke said. I didn't know Lance was presenting something, too.

'I haven't actually filmed mine yet,' said Lance, 'but my uncle in Auckland got a bit carried away . . . he offered to help me out with some footage. I know it's not exactly what we'd planned, because this isn't in my kitchen . . . it was at my cousin's wedding.'

'Woah!' everyone said at the same time when Lance's 360 shot appeared onscreen. The huge gathering of family and friends was incredible, with people in bright colours and more formal clothes. One man wore a cloak made out of feathers, and many guests had huge necklaces made of greenstone around their necks.

'This is at a *marae* in south Auckland,' Lance said, showing another picture. 'This is a *marae* I used to go to with my grandad. It's where we celebrate our Māori culture.'

'Our culture is everything,' said Jayden.

Jayden smiled at me, and I smiled back. Were we both saying sorry about the canteen incident in that moment?

I was just about getting my head around Jayden being nice to me when the even weirder thing happened, after class . . .

'Hey, Alice and Sami. Do you guys want to come to my place on Saturday? We're going to film my 360 shot,' Jayden said.

The invitation hung in the air, then Sami nudged me hard in the shoulder.

'Ow!' I said, scowling at Sami. 'I mean, yes, thanks, Jayden, that would be great.'

'We'll be there,' said Sami.

Who knows what the weekend will bring?

Bye for now,
Alice

SAVE FILE TAB 42

Alice Boghosian

Class 6O - Library writing project

Tuesday 9 March 2021

Dear Greta,

My phone is still confiscated, and so I haven't been able to speak to Anh. It's been stressing me out. How can I apologise to her or make it up to her?

'I think she has other things to worry about right now.' Sami hit me with a truth bomb today. 'I'm sure it's really not about the robot. She may not even be well enough to use it at the moment, Alice,' she said.

'Everything is going wrong . . .' I started.

'I wish you'd stop whinging,' Sami said. 'So, your grandmother borrowed your room. Big deal. You have a spare room. You don't have to share with your sister. And right now you get to see your grandmother every day, while she lives with you and recovers.'

I can't get Sami's face out of my head. She looked really upset, Greta. And, by the end of the day, she still hadn't said much to me. No matter how much I called after her, she didn't turn around on her way out of school. My stomach is in knots.

I thought I was a good friend, but I feel like I've managed to upset *everyone.*

Alice

SAVE FILE TAB 43

Alice Boghosian

Class 6O – Library writing project

Wednesday 10 March 2021

Dear Greta,

I'm worried that I'm not brave. I'm worried that I've hurt both my friends' feelings and I'm too chicken to even ask them.

I finally got my phone back, but it hasn't made any difference . . . There are no messages coming in, no silly emoji chats. Nothing. At all.

I need some of your nerve right now, Greta. How do you keep putting one foot in front of the other when it all feels so hard? I keep thinking about how fearless you were to set up your school strike outside the Swedish Parliament. You took a heroic step, not knowing how it would turn out.

I've been reading more of the books about you that Mrs Malouf gave me. It's amazing that you were inspired by kids who were taking a stance against guns, halfway across the world from you. The students from Marjory Stoneman Douglas High School in Florida, who courageously organised a march after a gun massacre at their school. It's so sad that they haven't changed the gun laws. Why won't grown-ups do something and actually listen to the students?

I'm trying to figure out how long you had to strike for, Greta, until the next Swedish election came around . . . Did it feel like a long time when you were there, striking?

I feel a bit miserable. My friends have gone quiet on me, and I miss them. I hate the idea that they're thinking badly of me.

Dad seems miserable, too. He can't even save the frogs in our local area, let alone whales in the Pacific. There's so much that needs to be done. Maybe, if us locals spoke up or protested about the freeway, we might be able to save the frogs? But how am I going to find the time to organise a protest when I still have to get the Food Fair organised, and somehow raise the money that I don't have to pay for the new iPad for Anh?

I don't know if I can help save the frogs. But I know what I can do. I'm going to channel you, Greta, and take *some* action, at least.

I'm going to call my friends. Right now.

Alice

SAVE FILE TAB 44

Alice Boghosian

Class 6O – Library writing project

Thursday 11 March 2021 (pm)

Dear Greta,

I'm feeling so much better about everything today! I nearly cried when Sami opened the door to her flat this afternoon after school. My big bunch of flowers for her got in the way of our hug, but it made us both laugh.

'I'm sorry, Alice!' she said, straightaway. And, just like that, a massive weight lifted off my chest.

'Me, too. I was being silly,' I said, stumbling around for words. I wish I was better at apologies. So, I grabbed Sami's hand. 'I'm sorry you miss your grandmother. You know you can visit Nene anytime you like, right?'

Sami's smile made me so happy! 'It's okay, Alice. I guess I was just missing my grandmother a bit too much.'

Walking into Sami's flat is like walking into a different world. There's the same old carpet and beige walls that we all have, but, somehow, it's mystical and magical and even smells mysterious.

Incredible rugs line the floors. They layer over each other until you can barely see the carpet. Unusual paintings in beautiful hues hang on every spare patch of wall. There is even a small pedestal with a statue on it. It looks like it belongs in a museum. The lounges don't look like anything out of Harvey Norman. They are deep and soft and you can sink into them and get lost in movies, as I have done a million times.

Sami's kitchen is a wondrous place, even though it's *tiny*. Where Anh's mum's kitchen is stark and bold, and ours is a bit messy, Sami's kitchen has ornaments and jars of things everywhere, even lined up on the windowsill. And today, I noticed a little bowl of rose petals, like something out of a magazine.

Sami's mum is elegant, with short black hair and thick eyeliner. She looks like she works at an art gallery, and Sami's home definitely could pass as one.

Mrs Hosseini kissed me three times, just like Nene does. Sami and her mum have been planning to make one of Sami's favourite meals for Sami's Food Fair contribution, a chicken and rice dish. It was tricky trying to get the shots to work in the small space. Three times, I had to shoo Mr Hosseini out of the kitchen because he kept getting in the way. (I think he wants to be famous, too.) But we figured it out in the end.

And Mrs Hosseini's rice! Mrs Hosseini uses both pistachios and slivered almonds on her rice or *polo*. Trust me, you'll never want to eat plain old rice ever again. Another secret is a dusting of sumac over the dish.

Best of all, though, was when Mrs Hosseini showed us her grandmother's – her *maman bozorg*'s – recipe book. It was covered in cloth and written in beautiful handwriting, and even though

I couldn't understand it, I knew it was really precious to her – and to Sami.

'I still use it all the time, when I forget things. This is the only thing I have left of her. I thank my stars every time I open it that I have it here with me,' she said. 'She made notes in it, like what specific rice to use. What seasons are best for certain fruits and vegetables.' Mrs Hosseini looked at the pages like she was remembering her own grandmother all over again. 'This is what we made today. *Khoresh-e Fesenjoon*, or Persian chicken stew with pomegranates and walnuts. One day, I'll pass this book and all its recipes on to Sami.'

And, Greta, my heart melted when I saw Sami's face. It was like she was only now realising that this was one day going to be hers.

After, Sami and I decided that that's how her family's Food Fair entry will open from the dropped pin on Iran; with the recipe book from a faraway land that is still so close in the hearts and minds of her family.

Books are amazing, especially the ones you make yourself.

Take care,
Alice

PS – there's still so much more that I have to do today, but I will keep you posted tomorrow on what happens next . . .

SAVE FILE TAB 45

Alice Boghosian

Class 6O – Library writing project

Friday 12 March 2021

Dear Greta,

Yesterday I put my Greta 'hat' on, because there was so much to do!

After Sami and I uploaded her photos to the Food Fair files, I headed to Anh's place. It had been on my mind the whole time I was at Sami's, and, as fun as Sami's was, there was still work to do! It was something I was nervous about, but going to see Anh immediately turned out to be the right decision.

Mrs Ha opened the door and drew me in for a hug. 'It's a good day, Alice! Anh will be so happy to see you.'

This time, I'd come armed with a box of chocolates. As I pushed open the door to Anh's bedroom, I found her not in bed, but sitting in an armchair looking out the window. She was attached to an oxygen tank, its tubes hooked over her ears and sitting under her nose. I was so happy to see her, but I tried to keep my emotions under wraps because seeing Anh like that was a little bit scary.

'Alice!' she said. 'Whassup?' Same old voice of Anh, but just not as much energy.

'I'm really sorry about the robot!' I wanted to clear the air as fast as I could. 'I'm saving up to pay for the new iPad for you for school,' I said in a rush. 'I've been grounded *for years*. Do you hate me?' I asked.

Anh laughed. 'Don't be ridiculous. You got me out of school.'

Huh. I'd never thought of it that way . . . *Phew!* I bent down to hug her in the armchair next to the window, then flopped on her bed and opened up the box of Cadbury's Favourites.

'Is there a Cherry Ripe in there?'

I fished around in the chocolate box.

'You're actually a lifesaver. With the robot out of order, it means no more classes, no more driving that thing around – and, you brought me chocolate! Mind you, if you could change this view, that'd be great.' Anh looked out across the rooftops of Melwood's unit blocks. Occasional treetops. Strings of washing hanging on people's balconies, and the grey fuzzy backdrop of the Blue Mountains.

'And you better stop buying chocolates so you can pay for my new iPad . . .' Anh laughed, but I could tell she didn't mean it. 'Nah,' she said. 'It's okay. I haven't been up for doing much, anyway. I haven't even opened any of the stuff that Ms O'Rourke sent me this week.' She pointed to a yellow padded envelope on her desk. 'Mum's not even making me do any schoolwork at the moment. Or Dad. That's when you know it's serious . . .'

We both munched in silence. I looked at the envelope. As much as it sounded like fun to miss school, I had to admit that being stuck in your bedroom alone all day would be pretty . . . uninspiring. Homeschooling during lockdown last year was hard enough!

'I just shot some pictures at Sami's place,' I said, desperate to change the subject. 'I thought, maybe, you might be up to making something for the Food Fair with your mum . . . ?' I took the 360 camera that Annie had lent me out of my bag. 'I'm going to leave this here for you, in case you feel up to it. No pressure, though.'

Anh just looked at it as she spoke, patting her oxygen tank on the stand next to her. 'Anywhere I go, this buddy has to come along, too. And, to be honest, Mum's kind of driving me crazy right now,' she said, and, at that moment, Anh's mum knocked and opened the door.

'Do you girls need anything?' She looked at us and the chocolate box.

'We're fine, Mum,' Anh said. But when Mrs Ha closed the door, she rolled her eyes. 'See what I mean? I can't get *five minutes* of peace and quiet.'

I'd never thought about that before. But I could imagine my parents doing exactly the same thing.

'I will do it, Alice,' she said. 'But find me another Cherry Ripe.'

Things are going to be okay.

Alice

SAVE FILE TAB 46

Alice Boghosian

Class 6O - Library writing project

Sunday 14 March 2021

Dear Greta,

I have to tell you about my crazy weekend, and I just can't wait until Monday – I need to get it all out now. Jayden's house was completely NOT what I was expecting . . . it was actually kinda fun . . .

Jayden's house was the loudest one on the street (no surprises there). There was music flowing out of the house that got even louder when we arrived at the front door – I wasn't even sure anyone would hear my knock above the party noise.

'*Kia orana*, girls. I'm Janice, Jayden's mum,' said a tall lady with black hair scooped high on her head and held in place by a frangipani flower pin. Looping around the top of her arm was an intricate band of tattoos, fine lines and solid blocks of black creating a mesmerising pattern. I had to stop myself from staring at it. It was beautiful.

'Hi, Mrs Tutai,' I said. 'I'm Alice, and this is Sami. We go to school with Jayden . . .'

'Yes, I remember you, Alice,' she said. But she was smiling this time. The last time we met, she'd been grim-faced, sitting opposite me and Mum, outside Mrs Abdullah's office. I'll admit I was freaking out a little bit at that point, feeling paranoid that Mrs Tutai hated me when I really wanted her to like me.

Mrs Tutai gestured us in, and we ended up on a quick tour through the house just to get to the kitchen. Jayden's house is *epic*. It is full to the brim of the most amazing things. There is an actual games room with a PS4, and full leather comfy chairs with headrests for gaming. The kitchen is huge, with every kind of gadget you can imagine on the counter. Nutribullet, coffee maker, you name it. There is even a whole room devoted to footy paraphernalia, stuffed with Tigers badges, pennants and framed pictures of players.

'You want a drink, girls?' Mrs Tutai asked Sami and me. 'We've got anything you like. OJ. Coke. Lemonade. Bubble water. Take your pick.'

I giggled in spite of myself. Jayden walked in and stopped when he saw us. Then it was Jayden's turn for a massive hug from Mrs Tutai. She planted a smacking kiss on the top of his head. 'So, you made up with Alice? Good work, JT,' his mum said. Jayden looked insanely embarrassed, and I couldn't help but giggle – not even *my mum* would do that to me.

'You know, Jayden hasn't stopped talking about this project,' Janice said. 'It's all he talks about.'

I was still processing his nickname – JT.

'*Mum*,' Jayden said. He looked like he wanted the floor to swallow him up.

Sami and I sneaked a glance at each other. Was she serious?

But Mrs Tutai went on. 'You wouldn't believe how much planning Jayden put into today. Facebook call-outs, church call-outs. It's a cast of thousands!' She looked at her son, pride written all across her face. 'And I'm so pleased you're working together now. That's the spirit,' she said.

I squirmed, but only a little bit. I unclenched my crossed fingers.

'So . . .' Jayden said. 'Everything's happening out the back. Come on out.'

"This house is so cool,' Sami said.

'It's home.' Jayden shrugged. But, Greta, it was a very *cool* home. I can guarantee Jayden doesn't sleep on an airbed . . .

We followed Jayden out the back, where the party was really underway. As we stepped out onto the deck, Sami and I realised we were only two of the entire neighbourhood that had been invited. Jayden sure had been busy . . .

'This backyard is awesome!' Sami said. 'And you know so many people!'

Everyone in the backyard was laughing, chatting and eating.

'It's COVID-safe, don't worry,' said Mrs Tutai, coming up behind us with cans of soft drink for us.

'It's not quite like being in New Zealand, but

it's the closest thing we could get,' Jayden said. 'It looks like the whole of Auckland is here, anyway,' he laughed.

'Seriously?' I said. 'Then Auckland must be a fun place.'

Jayden smiled at me. 'It is kinda cool . . .'

'Are you kidding me?' Sami said. 'This is the best party I've ever been to!'

That's when a delicious smell hit me. In the back corner of the yard was a huge spit with the biggest piece of meat I've ever seen turning over and over. Men and women were gathered around it, as if it were a shrine. A huge picnic table stood to the side of it, piled high with bread rolls and salads and condiments.

'Any excuse for a roast,' said a huge man in an All Blacks singlet top as he sidled up to Jayden. It was hard to miss the huge and detailed tattoos over almost every inch of his skin. I couldn't help but stare.

'This is my dad, Zane,' Jayden said.

'Did getting those hurt?' It just popped out of my mouth.

Jayden's dad laughed. 'They did, but they're part of me and my culture. So you don't really think about the pain, you think about the sacrifices your family has made. They tell the whole story of our family.'

'I'm going to get them, too, when I'm old enough,' said Jayden. 'Aren't I, Dad?'

'Yes, mate, you are.' Jayden's dad looked very proud. It was weird, Greta, but I hardly recognised Jayden on that day. He seemed like a completely different person here, at his home and around his family. Somehow less irritating . . .

'It's not quite an *umu*,' said Zane.

'What exactly is that?' I asked.

'It's an underground barbecue,' said Jayden. 'You cook a pig underground with coals for hours . . . It tastes delicious. But today, we've just done it on a spit. It still tastes pretty good.'

'It smells amazing. I'm starving,' I said, putting my stomach's rumbling into words.

'That makes two of us,' said a familiar voice next to us. It was Cortez, and he was wearing a T-shirt and shorts and there was no sign of his suit or tie. I guess teachers are . . . normal people, too.

'This is off the hook, Jayden!' Cortez surveyed the backyard scene from the deck.

'Check out the mandals,' Sami whispered to me, and I looked over at Cortez's feet. He looked like he was on holiday.

'Right, everyone,' boomed Jayden's dad. 'We're getting this photo, and then we're going to eat!'

There were whoops and hollers. Jayden and his dad were already standing on chairs in the middle of his backyard, surrounded by the huge throng of people.

'Alice, Sami, come down here,' Jayden called out. We put our drinks down and made our way to the centre shot, where Lance and Cortez were standing. Jayden handed the camera to his dad, then he jumped down to stand next to us.

'Everybody, say cheese!' Zane shouted.

'CHEEEEEEEEESE!'

On that command, we all jumped in the air while Jayden's dad swivelled on the chair to get the full 360 shot. And then, we tucked into the food.

Greta, it was like no other barbecue I've ever been to. In fact, I can still smell the mouthwatering pork, the delicious sauces, and I even tried the taro.

I can't wait to see the pic.

Bye for now,
Alice

SAVE FILE TAB 47

Alice Boghosian

Class 6O - Library writing project

Monday 15 March 2021

Dear Greta,

It was action stations at the computer room when I arrived at school this Monday morning. I was early – at 8:30am – but the gang was already there, and they were huddled around the computer.

After Jayden's barbecue, we'd all made plans to come in and upload the footage together. Plus, it was deadline day, so most students should have uploaded their 360 photos over the weekend.

'You didn't wait for me?' I asked, rushing in.

'Don't get upset, we're just uploading it now,' Jayden said. 'I couldn't wait to see it.'

'Great party,' I said. Another step in the peace deal between Jayden and me.

Jayden smiled, and then a picture popped onto the computer screen. 'Check this out, Alice! Monty Chu is basically a masterchef . . .'

'He can make noodles – and not the kind you rip open from a packet . . .' said Sami, while clicking 'Accept' on the smartboard to show Jayden's screen. Projected up on the board was a video file of Monty Chu making noodles with his mum. They started with just a small hill of flour and water on the counter, which they kneaded into a soft, white dough that they then rolled out into a thin sheet. By the end of the video, they were whirling the noodles around in the air, stretching them longer and longer . . . It looked like so much fun!

'Monty's kitchen is space age,' I breathed. 'Where's all the stuff?'

Our kitchen is crammed. Every time you open our pantry, something falls out. But Montgomery's kitchen is white on white, with shiny sharp appliances and a counter. Even with dough everywhere in the shot and hands deep in noodles, it could still be a picture out of a cookbook.

Raj's entry was also amazing. It showed him using a mortar and pestle to grind spices together into a paste for his tandoori chicken. We get our pastes from the supermarket in a jar, and I've never really thought about how to make them from scratch. But, I guess, that's the whole point of the virtual Food Fair.

Sami scrolled through file after file. There were Sudanese curries, Argentinian barbecues and Bangladeshi rice platters. And there was the one we'd been waiting for . . .

Jayden went a bit shy for some strange reason when his files came up on the screen. His 360 photo was full of colour. A swirl of people wearing huge smiles, and I instantly heard the music and smelled the food. But then I *actually* heard the music. Not only had Jayden created some recipe cards, he'd also added a song. I really didn't expect it. I may even have had some respect for it.

It's such a great feeling, seeing how amazing everything looks, and knowing that it's our hard work that's making it all possible. Almost everyone managed to upload their files, and the cameras are still being shared out across the Year Six students during this final week. We might just get this all finished in time.

Sami updated the home screen, sticking virtual pins on the world map in all the countries that the entries represented and celebrated. But there's one I know that's still missing – one from South Korea.

So far, there isn't an entry for Sweden, either. Do you have a favourite recipe to make, Greta? I know you're busy saving the world, but just something to think about. Right now, we're saving Harmony Day, and it feels exciting.

Yours,
Alice

SAVE FILE TAB 48

Alice Boghosian

Class 6O – Library writing project

Tuesday 16 March 2021

Dear Greta,

Breaking news. Nene wants to go *out* for dinner tonight. As in, not cook!?! She's booked a table somewhere and everything, and we all have to be ready at 6pm tonight. She's being so secretive about it! I'm just dying to know where we're going and what we'll be eating.

It's been ages since we went out for dinner – for a long time, we couldn't go out, thanks to COVID, and then, since Nene moved in, things have just been too busy. But, I figure, I must be back in the good books with everyone now . . .

I'll report back tonight.

Alice

SAVE FILE TAB 49

Alice Boghosian

Class 6O – Library writing project

Tuesday 16 March 2021 (pm)

Dear Greta,

Dinner was amazing! I'm still so full of dumplings in bed, I can hardly move. Nene took us to a Chinese restaurant called The Jade Lotus in Albion Vale. Apparently, it's her favourite restaurant.

Albion Vale is really busy, and Nene knows *everyone*. Once we'd parked, we followed Nene through the streets (none of us knew where The Jade Lotus actually was), and Nene seemed back in her element. She waved to the grocers as we walked past the shops that were still open and busy at six o'clock in the evening, with shoppers picking up the fruit and vegetables, weighing up their ripeness in their hands. She spoke with the spice shop owner, making us all stop and wait, and through the window I could see trays of spices, and little wooden shovels that you use to help yourself. On the counter were paper bags, and weighing scales.

There were parents pushing prams after dark. There were older men sitting outside drinking coffee. Nene waved to a couple, but she didn't stop to chat. There was a Turkish ice-cream parlour, with a long queue out the door (and you'll be pleased to know we stopped there for dessert on the way home).

Mum could not get over the cheap rolls of toilet paper that she somehow spotted from outside the mini-supermarket, and she lugged a whole 24-pack right into the restaurant with us. How embarrassing.

The Jade Lotus sat between Kebab King and The Maltese Falcon. Its restaurant window was covered in fairy lights and lace curtains. There were restaurant delivery drivers, on mopeds and electric bikes, hanging around in front of The Jade Lotus, waiting for orders. As we filed through the door, delivery vans trundled down the street behind us, double-parking in front of shops to unload more of the incredibly cheap toilet paper, groceries and flowers.

Inside, the restaurant was warm and bright, and Nene hugged everyone there like she'd known them a long time. It turns out, they all thought she had died (though no one said that specifically). Apparently, pre-heart attack, Nene ate at The Jade Lotus twice a week, and sometimes more. They knew her order off by heart. She'd been eating the same things for years – combination soup and fried rice.

Angela, the restaurant owner, brought dish after dish after dish to our table. I love Chinese food, but this dinner was *amazing*, and extra special, knowing that Nene was well enough to go out again (and I kinda liked that Nene and I loved exactly the same dishes). Annie and I were allowed to order soft drinks, and as many as we wanted. The owners were just so happy to have Nene back, they kept rushing back to check on us. Everyone was so happy. Even Annie and I, despite the fact that we were sitting next to each other, were happy.

But the best part was Nene's toast.

'To good health and family,' said Nene, and we all clinked glasses. And that's when Nene told us . . .

It seems the time has come. Nene is leaving us next week to go home. And what's weird is that, even though I didn't want her in my room in the beginning, I'm missing her already.

Love,
Alice

SAVE FILE TAB 50

Alice Boghosian

Class 6O – Library writing project

Wednesday 17 March 2021

Dear Greta,

Anh's in hospital. Ms O'Rourke told us in class today. And now I feel even worse about the following:

- Only managing to save about twenty dollars so far for her new iPad. Which means, if Mum and Dad hadn't loaned me the money for me to pay back, Anh would only be getting it by the time she finishes high school. I'm going to have to do a *lot* more chores . . . which also isn't great.
- Not being able to speak to or text Anh while she's in hospital. It's been *days*. It's really hard not hearing from her.

- The Harmony Day project. It's going really well, and I'm actually enjoying working on it (even if it's a bit stressful sometimes), but I feel a bit guilty when I know Anh is so sick and not able to do anything. Especially when I look at the absent pin in Vietnam on the world map home page.

I remember reading somewhere that you had to go into hospital one time when you were sick, Greta. Was it scary? I think it must have been so scary. I don't know how it feels to be in hospital, but when I think about Anh I worry that she is isolated, and like she's on her own in the world while going through something scary.

You and Anh might be really different, but you're definitely two of the strongest people I know.

Love and hugs to you, too, Greta,
Alice

SAVE FILE TAB 51

Alice Boghosian

Class 6O – Library writing project

Thursday 18 March 2021

Dear Greta,

Sami and I have invited ourselves over to Hannah's place, to help her with her Food Fair entry. She's the only person left in Year Six (except Anh) who hasn't sent something in. It's kind of urgent now that we get hers in before the deadline, and so we're going over tonight.

I did have lots of help from Nene and Annie with mine, and I helped Sami with hers, so it's time to help out Hannah. Now we know that she doesn't have any brothers and sisters, Sami and I said that we'd pretend to be her 'sisters' for a while.

I'll keep you posted!

Alice

SAVE FILE TAB 52

Alice Boghosian

Class 6O – Library writing project

Friday 19 March 2021

Dear Greta,

I'm so embarrassed about all the whinging I've done about Nene being in my room. Hannah barely *has* a room. And her house has no stuff in it. Like, *none.* Her parents work long hours, and the tower block walls are thin, and you can hear everything that the neighbours are watching on TV. It made me understand why Hannah had been avoiding doing a 360 video.

Hannah lives in a big block of units that sits right next to six other identical blocks of units on the edge of Melwood. The back fence of the building backs onto the freeway, and Mum said we could only walk there if Annie came with us, so she was along for the ride. There's no lift, and Hannah lives on the fifth floor. Even if Anh was well, there's no way her robot would have made it up all the stairs without us carrying it. We had so much stuff to carry, as it was.

Annie took her laptop, just in case Hannah didn't have a computer.

'I was going to make soup,' Hannah said, pointing at the bare kitchen where a few vegetables and a rice cooker sat on the counter.

It was a bit awkward, Greta. I'm pretty sure she'd never had any friends over from school before – and definitely hadn't had to cook a meal in front of them . . . And that's why I love Sami so much. She got glasses from Hannah's kitchen (without asking) and basically just bossed Hannah around until we were all laughing. I helped find some bowls in the cupboard, and Hannah lined up some unusual vegetables on the counter. '*Mu*. Radish,' she told me.

'Looking good for the shot,' I said, and everyone agreed.

'But it needs some action, don't you think, Hannah? Put us to work,' said Sami.

And so the three of us started to chop the veggies while Annie took a few photos, and Hannah finally relaxed.

But as soon as Hannah started cooking, it was obvious that she was the real star of the Year Six Food Fair all along, *because she actually knows how to cook.* We all thought we were going to help Hannah, but it turns out she was helping *us.*

Her entry for the Food Fair is going to be *so* good, Greta. I'm positive that the pictures will capture how in charge and confident Hannah was in the kitchen, and how she seemed to know exactly the right time to add each ingredient, and when to stir and when not to stir . . . just like Nene.

The meal Hannah made was a soup called *Janchi-guksu,* which was like nothing I've eaten before (Annie and I hadn't ever tried Korean food before yesterday). It was so tasty and delicious, with noodles and vegetables and even chopped-up boiled egg on top – which, of course, Hannah cooked just right.

I can follow instructions and pretend to cook (which is exactly what my entry is for the Food

Fair), but Hannah is so obviously the cook in her house that it kind of blew me away.

Imagine if we were having the *real* Food Fair. Hannah would have had the most popular stand, I reckon.

I'm pretty sure that we were the first guests in Hannah's home. Sami, Annie and I all agreed that we definitely won't be the last.

Love,
Alice

PS – Guess what? Hannah's name is actually *Ha-na*, in Korean. She wrote her name down in *hangul,* which is the Korean alphabet, and she helped us to practise saying her name correctly . . . I wish she'd told us sooner that we'd all been pronouncing it wrong!

SAVE FILE TAB 53

Alice Boghosian

Class 6O - Library writing project

Monday 22 March 2021

Dear Greta,

Do you want the good news . . . or the wild news?

This morning, I found myself in Mrs Abdullah's office for the second time in a couple of weeks. But this time, she was so happy with me it's not funny (even if she can't bring herself to say it out loud). I squished into her vinyl couch with Sami and Jayden and Lance, and watched Cortez show her our website, now that it was finished and live. The home page map is pockmarked with a hundred and fifty pins all over the world. Sami did a really great job of designing it.

Mrs Abdullah nudged Cortez out the way, and

clicked excitedly, here and there, all over the world, looking at everyone's entries.

Drumroll please . . . she loved them.

She happened to click on Jayden's entry in the Cook Islands, and his epic backyard shot filled the screen. Even though I'd seen it already, the energy and excitement from that afternoon in Jayden's backyard pulsated from the photo. You could almost smell the meat on the roast. Mrs Abdullah insisted on zooming in on aspects of the photo. I could see my face and Sami's wedged in between the backyard crowd.

'Glad to see you patched things up,' she said, glancing pointedly at Jayden and me over her shoulder. 'It's clear you've been working very hard behind the scenes,' she said. And she looked very approvingly at us all still squished into her sofa. It's a lot better than her angry face, Greta.

Lance's picture came up, too, and it was out of control. His cousin and her new husband had taken a 360 shot at their wedding in Auckland, which captured hundreds of guests during a ceremonial dance.

My own entry might not be the flashiest, but I'm still proud of it. And I know Sami loves hers, too. I guess all of our entries mean something personal to us. Getting to see everyone else's is like looking into a little window of their world.

'Now, I don't want you to get overexcited, team,' Cortez said, 'but we've had some media requests from the local TV stations about covering the online Food Fair.'

'I don't need to tell you how important this moment will be,' Mrs Abdullah said, once again glancing at her wall of fame – students who had made the big time in the newspapers. Was it entirely possible that we could join Annie on that wall?

Mrs Abdullah's eyes fell on me. Again.

'Alice, since this project began with your initial idea, I'd like you to represent Year Six at Melwood Public School on *Brekky HQ*,' she said.

I think our jaws all dropped at that point. Mine actually hit the floor. Only a few weeks ago, I was in this office, sweating over the possibility of being suspended. And now . . .

'You mean . . . THE *Brekky HQ?* The one everyone in Australia watches?' I asked, my voice cracking.

Now I really need to channel some of your power, Greta!

I'm going to be on TV!

Alice

PS – Happy Harmony Week!

SAVE FILE TAB 54

Alice Boghosian

Class 6O - Library writing project

Tuesday 23 March 2021 (pm)

Dear Greta,

Today has been a blur – since the time Mum dropped me off at school this morning and we saw the TV vans parked outside school, to right now, back in my own bed in my own room, where I'm still buzzing . . . I have to write to you just to let out the insanity of today!

Annie and Dad had wanted to come to school with me and Mum this morning, but their excitement had been making me even more nervous, so I'd ignored their pleas and dragged Mum out to the car to drive me so I could get some calm.

My phone pinged. It was a text message from Nene.

I can't wait to watch you on TV. x Nene.

Mrs Ha had also sent me a text from Anh, wishing me luck and lots of thumbs-up emojis! I pocketed my phone as we turned into my school's street, and that's when Mum started acting all silly, especially when we saw Peter Minchin, the reporter from *Brekky HQ*, walking into the school front gate with a camerawoman next to him.

Do you play it cool, Greta, when you meet famous people (which I know you do – all the time)? Because I just couldn't, and Mum wasn't helping. Everything about Peter Minchin just made my legs turn to jelly and my brain to mush.

Peter Minchin seemed a lot smaller in person than he does on TV, with much higher hair than I'd expected. Big TV vans with satellites on the roofs were parked on the inside of the school gate.

'Alice, this is so exciting!' Mum pulled the car into the kerb in the kiss-and-ride section. She leaned over, gave me a hug and a searching look that seemed to peer into my soul. 'I'm so proud of you, Alice. For everything.' She may even have wiped away a tear. It was *quite* dramatic. And it didn't help with my nerves one bit. Instead, I panicked. Mum, Dad, Annie, Nene and even Mrs Ha and Anh seemed very invested in me being interviewed on TV. I could not screw this up.

Mum pulled herself together, straightening up in her seat, while I remained frozen with nerves. 'Just one selfie,' she promised. 'You look great!'

I had attempted to tame my hair this morning, but, as usual, instead of lying flat and glossy, my curls were wild and springy in Mum's photo. Annie had told me to 'lean in' to it, just like she does. I'm not sure I'll ever 'lean in' to my wild hair, but I can hope to one day be the zen-master that Annie is . . .

Then Sami was at my car window, almost beating it down, feverishly urging me to come in the gates. She briefly waved to Mum before almost yanking me out of the car and in through the school gates.

The library was barely recognisable. Mrs Malouf had worked wonders. It sparkled, and there wasn't a book out of place. Even our writing project looked enticing. I saw you out of the corner of my eye on the wall, Greta – maybe you would be good inspiration for today! And in the middle of it all, almost unrecognisable, was Cortez, in a suit that looked one size too small for him. Lance and Jayden had scrubbed up, too, wearing the emerald-green blazers that we all hated.

It was hot. There were cameras and blazing lights and none of the windows were open. Cortez mopped sweat from his brow with a wrinkled handkerchief. 'What a day for the AC in the library to go on the blink,' he said, wiping his upper lip.

I was already sweaty with nerves, even without the hot day. I realised my armpits were overly moist, and I could feel sweat running down the back of my uniform.

Sami and I wound our way through the hot, bright lights on stands. The camerawoman I'd seen walking with Peter Minchin was setting up her tripod and untangling cables and plugging them in to lots of different black boxes.

'Check out all the gear,' Sami breathed. 'Imagine what we could produce with this – maybe the Food Fair online is just the beginning!'

I felt sure that Sami was destined to become a TV producer.

In the corner, Peter Minchin was scrolling through his phone. He had his back to us, but I'd recognise those bleached-blond gelled tips anywhere.

'Time to get mic-ed up,' said a voice beside me. It was the camerawoman. 'You're Alice, aren't you?'

I nodded. Words actually failed me.

'I'm going to get you to pop this on your collar,' she said, handing me a small microphone on a clip. 'You're going to be fine, Alice!' But I wasn't fine. I couldn't get the microphone clip to work and hang on my school uniform properly. Thankfully, Sami saw it all and came to my rescue. Sami's smile and her hands on my shoulders, like a netball coach calming her team at the grand final, made me feel a bit better.

Mrs Abdullah stood in the corner, talking with Peter Minchin. I took deep breaths and tried to look down at the microphone. Was it loud? Could Australia hear my deep breathing?

Then Peter Minchin wheeled around and shone his brilliance on me. Everything about him was dazzling – from his whitest of white teeth to the shiny shellac of his hair gel that was holding his hair up and adding a lot of height. His suit was tight, and his shirt so white and starched that it seemed radioactive. And, in a strange way, he calmed me down. I could only focus on him, not the bundle of knots in my tummy.

'And you're Alice!' he said, warmly, coming up to my side.

I liked him immediately. Probably because we were almost the same height.

'That's me,' I said, looking at Cortez for inspiration . . . If I couldn't even think of an answer to my own name here, I was going to be in trouble. But Cortez looked as tongue-tied as I felt.

'And what's your surname, just so I get it right?'

'Alice Boghosian. That's B-O-G-H-O-S-I-A-N,' I told him. I cringed in anticipation of him botching my name. What if he ended up calling me *Bogus*?

'Okay, great!' he said, writing it down on his little notepad, which he'd whipped out from his pocket. 'That's Armenian, right?' he said, looking at me. 'Gotta be! Ends in "ian".'

I nodded. I was actually shocked! How on earth did he know about Armenian names! 'Bingo!' I said. A phrase I have never, ever used in my life before (live TV does weird things to people).

'I must be part Armenian then,' said Cortez, holding out his hand to Peter Minchin. '*Ian* Cortez, Year Six adviser. Alice is part of the amazing team of students who put this idea together. They're all great students, and here's the rest of the stellar team now,' he said. Suddenly, I found that Jayden, Lance and Sami were close by. It felt good to have my crew near me.

But I couldn't shake the feeling that I was an impostor. I wasn't one of the best students. I was the student that got into a fight and broke her sick friend's robot . . . remember? But even Jayden gave me a thumbs-up and a big smile.

'Ha ha,' Peter Minchin chuckled, before looking at me. 'My neighbour's Armenian.' He leaned closer, and said in a conspiratorial tone, 'Anoush Hagopian. Do you know her?' He looked at me, with his piercing blue eyes, bleached-blond hair and bronzed god skin.

It's a shame. He was doing so well, I thought.

'Ha – just kidding,' Peter Minchin said, and then touched an earpiece in his ear.

'Wait. What . . .?' Before I had time to smile, let alone make a quip back, he'd nodded to the voice in his ear, and looked pointedly at Cortez and me.

'Quick, Alice – put this on.' It was Mrs Christodoulou at my side. She handed me a green blazer. *Not another piece of second-hand clothing from my favourite office lady . . .*

'I've never worn a blazer in my life,' I whispered to Peter. 'Plus, it's forty degrees in here . . .' I reluctantly took the blazer and saw Mrs Abdullah's approving smile. There was no way I was getting out of wearing it.

'We're going to be on in thirty seconds,' Peter said, touching his earpiece, looking at me and Cortez while I fought my arms into the blazer.

That's when I couldn't remember anything I had planned to say. The phrases I had rehearsed were absolutely nowhere to be found . . .

'Cortez, right?' Peter Minchin looked at my teacher and straightened his tie, and the girl with the headphones came and smoothed out Peter's shoulder pads that were stretched across his shoulders. She then whipped out a small pad of bronzer. Finally, she patted down all the sweat off his face, and dusted him with even more powder.

She looked at Cortez's and my sweaty faces and whipped out another make-up case, blotting our faces, too.

'Ten seconds,' the camerawoman said, just as a lady in a big pink jacket and skirt bustled in. I recognised her immediately. Mayor Pennyworth. She moved quickly, pushing Cortez out of the way and out of shot. It was so rude!

'Got wind of this,' the mayor said, arriving in a cloud of hairspray mixed with perfume.

My throat constricted, and literally all I wanted to do was a loud, hacking cough. Which wouldn't have been socially acceptable and definitely not right for breakfast TV.

'Wouldn't miss it for the world,' she continued, holding out her palm to Cortez for his earpiece, and hastily grabbed his lapel microphone, which she promptly attached to her fuchsia suit jacket.

The mayor's heavy brass mayoral necklace jangled, and she turned to give me the most insincere smile in the world.

I looked at Cortez in alarm. His confusion mirrored mine. Poor Cortez looked like a hostage in a negotiation gone wrong.

'Alicia, is it?' The mayor barely looked at me, her bronzed face shiny with sweat.

'Alice,' I corrected her.

And that's when things went off the rails. Politicians should never

SAVE FILE TAB 55

Alice Boghosian

Class 6O - Library writing project

Tuesday 23 March 2021 (pm)

Dear Greta,

Sorry! I hit send before I meant to!

Politicians should never provoke children, animals or anyone, really. I don't need to tell you that, Greta.

'With me here at Melwood Public School this morning is Year Six student, Alice Boghosian,' Peter said, swinging into action. He said my name perfectly, and for a moment I forgot about the lights and the fact that I was live on national television, wearing an insanely hot jacket with sweat rolling down my temples.

'Why don't you tell us about your recent project, Alice?' The reporter looked at me intently, smiling his encouragement. I took a deep breath. I wanted to sound confident and happy, even if I didn't feel it. I was just about to reply when the mayor cut in.

'This is a marvellous expression of community, Peter,' she purred, pulling the camerawoman in her direction. 'Simply wonderful effort from Alicia here,' she put a reassuring hand on my shoulder, '. . . and the Melwood Public School students.'

I coughed. 'It's *Alice*,' I said.

'That's what I meant,' she barged on. 'Taking Harmony Day online this year is simply *wonderful*.' Mayor Pennyworth beamed, as if it had been *her* idea all along.

'And what about you, *Alice*?' Peter Minchin again asked me, looking pointedly past the mayor and in my direction.

'I –'

'The innovation is simply brilliant,' the mayor cut in again. 'Family and extended community can really get together with these new technologies –'

If Peter Minchin was actually losing it behind his breakfast-show microphone, he was very good at keeping his cool. Maybe his eyebrow quirked up a little. Me? I was boiling, ready to pop!

'My council and I really want to bring the community together –'

And that was it. I'd had enough, Greta. Sick of the mayor talking over me. All I'd wanted to do was say my piece about the Food Fair project. But thanks to the mayor, I unfortunately veered off course . . .

'You know,' I cut in, in the most polite way possible, '*students* are the ones doing something great for the community, by using *their* ideas. You should see what my friends here in Year Six have created. Harmony Day has always meant so much to everyone, and that's why every single Year Six student has sent in the most amazing recipes from their own kitchens! We've built an online world to share all this and to celebrate – hopefully, it brings us all together, even if it's only virtually . . .' I said.

'We'd like to thank everyone involved, especially our behind-the-scenes team: Sami, Lance, Jayden and Cortez – I mean, *Mr* Cortez . . . Everyone worked really hard.' I snuck a look at the rest of my team off to the side of the camera, and imagined Anh standing there, too, in the place that she *should* be, not stuck in a hospital bed. Which gave me an idea . . . 'I also want to say hi to our friend Anh, who is in hospital right now . . .'

I ploughed on. My torrent was turning into a complete landslide, which wasn't over yet . . .

'Kids have really good ideas, Peter,' I said, looking down the barrel of the camera. Peter nodded enthusiastically next to me. 'At Melwood, we used this chance to change things up and do things differently. The world is changing, and we have the chance to start making good decisions. Are you going to start saving our community, too, Mayor Pennyworth?' I asked, swinging around to her.

The mayor's eyes hardened behind her fixed smile. She clearly wasn't used to people talking back to her. Or kids asking difficult questions. Her eyes were like diamond lasers cutting through my soul. But, for some reason, her hard stare made all my nerves disappear, and I found I had a lot more to say . . .

'Because there's a lot *we* want you to do for *us*. For instance, instead of creating a new freeway exit into Melwood, why don't you save the wetland reserve, like you promised? We'd be saving the endangered Green and Golden Bell Frog, as well as preserving an ecosystem for future generations.' I crossed my fingers behind my back, hoping that was the right name of the species.

The mayor drew in breath as I finished. Her poker face slipped. Her eyes bulged.

Sweat ran down the back of my uniform and under the collar of the blazer at my neck. I squirmed inside, and was grateful when Peter Minchin wrapped it up . . .

'Thank you, ladies. It was great to have a sensible debate on some serious issues. Maybe we'll get you back on to discuss them, Mayor?' But before the mayor had a chance to speak, Peter Minchin said, brightly, pointing at the camera, 'Hi Anh! Get well soon. Now, it's back to you in the studio!'

There was deathly silence for about twenty seconds. That's when I heard Cortez clap quietly from behind. I turned and saw, behind him,

Mrs Abdullah's face contorted into something between pain and pride. My stomach was flip-flopping. Had I done the right thing? It felt like it. And it was so exciting that Peter Minchin had given Anh a shout-out live on air. In front of the whole country.

Then the hot lights switched off around me, and the camerawoman took the camera pack off her shoulder and began packing up equipment. Just like that, it was over. My moment of fame and glory.

'That was so incredible, Alice!' said Sami, almost skipping across the library towards me, followed by Jayden and Lance.

'You told the mayor off!' Jayden sounded impressed.

'Unreal, Alice!' said Lance, high-fiving me.

'Thank you so much, Alice!' Peter was saying to me as the mayor stalked off in a huff, demanding a bottle of water from her assistant.

'How did that happen?' A voice cut in my ear, just as I'd started to take off my lapel microphone. Peter Minchin and I looked at each other. The mayor had forgotten to take off her microphone, so everything she was saying came in loud and clear through our headpieces.

'Kids these days have too much to say.' The mayor seethed at her assistant. 'Get that kid out of my face, and let's get out of here,' we heard her say. 'This school is a joke!'

The mayor and her assistant were nearly out the door when I caught up to them and tapped her on the shoulder.

'You might want to take off your lapel microphone,' I said, helpfully. 'We're still getting everything you're saying.' I tapped on my ear.

Her face? Priceless.

It was a sweet, sweet moment, Greta.

Kids 1 – Politicians 0

Night night! Sweet dreams!
Alice

SAVE FILE TAB 56

Alice Boghosian

Class 6O – Library writing project

Wednesday 24 March 2021

Dear Greta,

Going viral is very strange. It feels like flying. I don't know which device to look at, which clip to watch. I'm currently flicking between this email on the iPad and YouTube. I still cringe when I hear my voice. (Do I really sound like that?) I'm sick of looking at my own face. But, somehow, I can't get enough. Do you ever feel that way?

Annie has cut a *gif* of Peter Minchin saying: *Hi Anh! Get well soon Hi Anh! Get well soon Hi Anh! Get well soon Hi Anh! Get well soon Hi Anh! Get well soon Hi Anh! Get well soon Hi Anh! Get well soon* with me grinning in-shot. It only gets irritating after you've watched it twenty-five times.

But Mum and Annie still laugh every time they hear it. Does your sister Beata do the same, and watch your stuff over and over?

'Alice, you're trending,' Annie said, coming into my room this morning to sit on my bed. She can't believe it, and neither can I. 'What's the deal with the blazer, though? It's slightly huge . . .'

I nodded. I had smelled like mothballs again . . . but I don't think anyone else really noticed.

On camera, however, the jacket looked dazzlingly emerald and ridiculously massive on me. Everything on TV is amplified – from the bright bold green of my humungous blazer to the shiny nose of the mayor, the pink of her jacket reflecting her own pink face. The only person that looked completely normal was Peter Minchin.

'I've played the clip a thousand times,' said Mum over breakfast. 'You wiped the floor with the mayor, Alice!' Nene and Mum watched the phone again and again. While I'm finding it excruciating to watch the clip, I'm still proud of what I said . . . and surprised at myself for doing it.

Best of all has been Annie's reaction – she is so

impressed with what I did! She said she could never have done that. It makes me feel even happier that I stood up for us!

'Well done, *jan*,' said Nene, pulling me in for a hug. She's back at our place for celebrations with the local 'TV celeb'. ☺ 'I never watched *Brekky HQ* before today, but that Peter Minchin seems all right!'

Oh! And apparently, the video has been doing the rounds at Dad's work. Last night, Dad came home, and joked about being 'related to someone very influential'.

'You mean me, of course,' said Annie, joking.

But no. He meant me! I couldn't help but glow with . . . I don't even know what this feeling is. Is it pride? Whatever it is, it feels good, Greta!

'Because of the media interest around the endangered frogs and the freeway exit, we may have a second ray of hope,' said Dad.

'That's awesome news,' said Annie.

'Don't get too excited. It doesn't mean anything yet. But it looks like the council might re-look at the freeway extension at their next meeting. Thanks, Alice,' Dad said, looking relieved.

But I couldn't take *all* the credit . . . 'Don't thank me, Dad. Thank Greta. She's the one who started *everything*,' I said. And I meant it!

Thanks, Greta!

Alice

SAVE FILE TAB 57

Alice Boghosian

Class 6O – Library writing project

Thursday 25 March 2021 (pm)

Dear Greta,

If I thought that the beginning of this week was *good,* that becoming a short-term TV star and internet sensation was *fun,* then today beat everything *hands-down.* Not only did Sami and I get to finish school for the day at lunchtime, we also got to see Anh!!!

Doctor Freya, Anh's doctor, said that Anh's getting better, and that she might even be able to come back to school soon – for real! But right now, we're allowed to visit her in the hospital, and so Mr Hosseini picked Sami and I up from school before lunchtime, and drove us there.

Before we had even walked into her special

glass-walled room, we could see Anh mocking us for wearing our school uniforms to the kids' hospital.

The three of us didn't stop chatting the entire time we were there. We didn't even notice the babyish rainbows on the wall this time, or the giant teddies waving from every nurse's station.

We caught Anh up on all the gossip, but it turns out her mum had beaten us to it. How is it possible that Anh knows *more* about what's happening at school than we do?

Lots of love,
Alice

PS – I've now raised forty dollars towards the iPad, and Nene snuck me an extra twenty, which I added to the piggy bank, too.

SAVE FILE TAB 58

Alice Boghosian

Class 6O – Library writing project

Friday 26 March 2021 (pm)

Dear Greta,

I've been missing Nene, more than I ever missed my room. I've even started to miss how she folded our washing, which somehow kept out all the creases . . . and this is exactly what I found her doing when I got home this afternoon . . .

But Nene was folding *her* things up and putting them away in her orange-wheeled suitcase. I knew that this was the last batch of stuff that Nene had left at our house . . .

'Do you need help?' I asked, after tapping on the door. My bedroom door.

Nene shook her head. 'You know, I really didn't want to stay here,' she said. 'I like my own space.

I have my routines. I like my house. Mostly, I didn't want to ever think of myself as sick, or weak.'

'I've never thought of you that way,' I said, and I honestly never had. Nene never seemed weak or vulnerable, not even that first day she had come home from hospital and I'd found her wearing my clothes in my bed.

'That's good. But when I got here, I didn't feel great, if I'm being honest. I'm not one for lying down and taking naps.'

I didn't know what to say to that. Grandmothers take naps, and they should be allowed to. 'Shall I pack these?' I asked, running a finger along the frame of a photo of Annie and I as little kids. I collapsed the photos gently, and gathered up the statues of the Virgin Mary. I rolled up the doilies as I went.

'Put them in there,' Nene said, pointing at a towel laid out at the end of my bed.

'Annie and I will come and visit you,' I said. 'There are so many more recipes I want to learn.'

Nene smiled. 'Next week, you come straight from school and we'll get started,' she said. 'You know that you can walk to my place from school, don't you?'

I'd never thought about it, but her house *is* close to school. That made me feel a little bit better about her going home, knowing she was still close. That's when she put her small, smooth wrinkled hand in mine and squeezed.

I didn't want her to go, but this wasn't about me. It was time for her to get back to her own life again.

Love,
Alice

SAVE FILE TAB 59

Alice Boghosian

Class 6O - Library writing project

Monday 29 March 2021

Dear Greta,

I've been thinking a lot about cicadas today (they're so loud at the moment, it's hard to ignore them). I found a shell this morning, at eye level on the tree at the bus stop. I plucked it off, looking at the delicate brown case, cradling it in my hand. Not long ago, a black prince or a greengrocer cicada shed this skin.

The nymphs live underground for years, emerging when the time is right. Had this cicada been waiting for the bushfire seasons to pass and the temperatures to cool? We're now in *La Ninã* – a wet and rainy summer, and that has made it a Cicada Year. If temperatures rise higher, cicadas might not make it.

I can't imagine a future without cicadas, or wetland frogs. They are the soundtrack to summer that I couldn't live without. They have always been a part of my life – and they need to be around for the next generations, too. I couldn't put the cicada shell in my pocket, or in my bag without crushing the shell, so I put it back on the tree.

I spent a whole morning over the weekend moving my stuff back from the sunroom into my bedroom. Nene is back in her own home now, with all her things. Her heart has repaired. But my heart is a bit sad. My old bedroom, I don't even want it back. My pink vanity is still bare, with the marks created by Nene's pictures still showing in the layer of dust.

I would have happily stayed in the sunroom a bit longer.

The house feels empty, and the kitchen is boring.

I'm not even feeling very inspired by this writing project in the library today. I'm just feeling . . . sad. (Sorry if you're reading this, Mrs Malouf. And sorry to you, too, Greta.)

Love,
Alice

SAVE FILE TAB 60

Alice Boghosian

Class 6O – Library writing project

Tuesday 30 March 2021

Dear Greta,

Mrs Malouf caught me dropping off the stack of books on you into the returns chute this afternoon. I'd been hoping to get in and out of the library without bumping into her and acknowledging what has been going on – that I've been writing to a world leader in the vain hope that she (you) might write back, while a teacher reads everything I write.

For some reason, I didn't really think about it while I was writing the emails. But now, it's the last week of term, and I'll be graded on the project, and it's made me realise that that means Mrs Malouf will be reading *everything* . . . and so my days of writing to you are just about over, Greta. I'm not sure how I feel about that.

'Did you enjoy those books, Alice?' Mrs Malouf had me cornered, and I somehow felt like I was being tested.

'Yes,' I said, carefully.

'I think you're a natural writer,' went on Mrs Malouf. To avoid looking at her, I stuck my hand down the chute to fish out a book that shouldn't have been in there. Mrs Malouf's own book.

'I think this one is yours,' I said, pulling her book from the pile. 'This one was actually my favourite.'

'I'm glad you liked that one,' she said.

'Your picture reminded me of Greta,' I said, turning to the pictures of the 'No Nukes' protest, and the newspaper clipping that showed Mrs Malouf holding up the protest sign.

'Oh, goodness,' she said, peering closely at the yellowed piece of newspaper. 'I'd forgotten that was in there.'

'It must have meant a lot to you at the time, to protest against the nuclear-bomb testing,' I said.

'It did,' said Mrs Malouf. 'I thought it was important to stand up to the powers that be. I thought the Australian government wasn't doing enough to protect the environment and our precious Pacific. My friends and I felt that we had to take matters into our own hands, to make a statement to force them to do something about it.'

'Just like Greta,' I said.

She smiled. 'Just like Greta. But don't think *you* aren't making changes, Alice. The work you have all achieved with the Food Fair is just fantastic. I'm really proud of you, and the way you handled that TV interview . . .'

'Thanks, Mrs Malouf,' I said, but my mind was whirring. The words *take matters into our own hands* were rippling across my mind. Suddenly, I had a huge urge to talk to Sami, Jayden and Lance.

I raced out the library door. Then back in. There was something I needed to lock in.

'Yes, Alice?' Mrs Malouf asked.

'Are you free on Friday morning, say, eight o'clock?' I asked.

She thought about it, a strange look coming over her face. 'I think so,' she said.

'Great,' I said.

I heard her calling my name as, this time, I made it out the door. But I didn't look back.

The time is now, Greta.

Alice

SAVE FILE TAB 61

Alice Boghosian

Class 6O – Library writing project

Tuesday 30 March 2021

Dear Greta,

Sorry for being so cryptic earlier. I've had an idea burning away inside of me all day. It's not quite concrete yet, but I do know that I need my friends' help on this one.

I thought Year Six was going to be different, but I didn't expect that it was going to be quite *this* different . . .

For a start, I never thought I would be sorry to say goodbye to extra schoolwork, which is exactly what happened today.

'Sadly, the time has come for us all to return to regular programming,' said Cortez, while looking as glum as us that the *STEM 4 SCHOOLS* kits were moving on to their next home, ready to start Term 2 in a new school.

It also means that the extra freedom we had is over. We all have to go back to regular class full-time, so today we made sure that we made our free time at Cortez's demountable last. Cortez was also packing up. He's moving on to become Acting Principal while Mrs Abdullah goes on study leave.

'I've liked coming here,' said Jayden. 'We got to have fun.'

'My mum's really happy with me,' said Lance. 'Looks like I might be going to Whitlam High with you guys, after all,' he said, looking at Jayden and me.

I never thought I'd say this, Greta, but I'm glad Lance isn't being sent to St Leo's Bad Boy Reform School. (Yet.)

'I'm going to miss checking our numbers,' said Sami.

Because of so much media around our Food Fair project, the number of visitors to our website has been extreme. I must admit, I've become addicted to watching the number of views climb, too – Sami showed me how to get into the back end of the website system to do stats. It's completely mesmerising watching the numbers grow and grow. It's much higher than if we'd just held the ordinary Food Fair on our school grounds. Crazy, right?

Now that it's over – the launch, the media, our team – I have been trying to push away this feeling . . . that it's all over. It just can't be . . . not yet?

We all watched the courier load the huge black cases holding the precious equipment into his van. Sweating, the deliveryman rolled them out of the demountable and down the steps. *Thunk, thunk, thunk.* It wasn't quite like releasing doves into the sky, but they were heading off to a new home.

'Wonder where these are heading next,' Sami said, sticking one final sticker on the *STEM 4 SCHOOLS* cases. We'd created a team sticker that read:

This kit has been around the world (and to Melwood Public School).

'Do you think they'll have as much fun as we did?' Sami asked.

'No chance,' said Jayden. 'Are you sure there isn't something else here for us to do, or help with?'

Jayden looked around the computer room. Lance dawdled. Sami and I lingered. I looked around the room. It was semi-clean, with real workstations. For a while, it had returned to being a classroom and a hive of activity, rather than just a computer graveyard. I felt like we had achieved something really great – and that now, anything was possible.

'Don't get any ideas, you guys.' Cortez was stern, but I could still see a smile on his face.

'That's not what Greta would say,' I murmured.

'Greta who?' Jayden asked.

'*The* Greta. Greta Thunberg,' I said. 'There's always something that she's doing. For the world. For the climate. For us.'

'And how does she affect us, exactly?' Lance said.

'Remember those frogs I mentioned in the interview on *Brekky HQ* . . .?'

And that's when the next great Alice Plan was hatched.

I'll fill you in soon, Greta.

Yours,
Alice

SAVE FILE TAB 62

Alice Boghosian

Class 6O - Library writing project

Wednesday 31 March 2021 (pm)

Dear Greta,

This afternoon, I jumped off the bus at an earlier stop. Annie was already waiting for me. And we did something we'd never done before. We walked for twenty-five minutes over to Albion Vale to Nene's house.

The outskirts of Melwood look just like the inskirts – flat, organised streets. As we headed out beyond the shops and crossed over the freeway on the footbridge, I felt like an explorer crossing a new frontier. From up here, we could see Ha-na's block of units, and I realised how close we actually lived to each other. Close enough that I could definitely hang out with Ha-na more often after school (although I won't make her cook for me next time ☺).

For a while, Annie and I stood over the huge B-doubles as they hurtled their way down to Canberra, standing in the windy wake of their slipstreams. The covered footbridge absorbed the huge weights hurtling past us, but you could *feel* the rumbling power of the huge vehicles bellowing below our feet.

Annie and I had argued with Mum and Dad about the walk to Nene's. It felt good (but strange) to be arguing on the same side of the fence as Annie, for the first time in forever.

Finally, they had let us win, though I'm sure somewhere in my backpack they'd put a transmitter, following our every move. But the footbridge was built for exactly this reason – to cross the freeway safely.

When we got down into Albion Vale, it was quiet again. Nene's neighbourhood is filled with tiny old Federation workers' cottages, most of which are being renovated, just like on *The Block*. Melwood is neat and orderly, being an old defence suburb, but Albion Vale is the opposite – winding streets and sprawling yards.

Annie and I felt like impostors as we pulled the gate closed behind us and walked down the side footpath to Nene's place. We always found it a bit strange that she lives behind some other family's house. It must be weird for them, too, to see other kids come into their yard, but they have only ever been nice to us. A huge jasmine bush was in full bloom, wrapped around the staircase leading up to Nene's front door, which is painted a deep, pomegranate red.

Something smelled delicious.

Then Nene was at the front door, drawing us both in for a cuddle. (Weird, but I had a few tears that I blinked away.) She was wearing her usual blue-and-white-striped apron, which is so big on her tiny frame that it looks like a dress.

Nene had invited us for afternoon tea, and she'd already laid out on her tiny dining table (a coffee table in disguise, thanks to a white cloth) her special Jerusalem pottery cups and plates – and even cups and saucers next to small jars of little goodies. A big vase of jasmine overflowed, its delicate pink flowers spilling onto the table.

Annie and I dumped our bags on Nene's bed inside her neat little bedroom, so that they were out of the way. I noticed that her photos were back in their rightful places. Her own parents watched over her and the room. I wondered what they would make of Annie and me . . . Would they have noticed a change in me from when they left my bedroom to now . . .? I feel like there is a change in me that's just bursting out for the world to see. A change that makes me feel good and scared at the same time.

Nene's rosaries were back, too, hanging from their rightful knobs on her dresser, and the doilies looked much more at home here than they ever did in my bedroom.

'Chai gooz-em?' Nene asked. *Do you want tea?*

Annie and I nodded. Nene boiled the electric kettle for our tea, but she made herself Turkish coffee in a small *jezveh,* and she poured us each our piping hot drinks. It feels special to drink tea in this way, in her special china. And I must admit,

I only ever drink tea at Nene's, when it's rich and sweet.

'Your lessons begin now,' Nene said. 'It's very important that you learn how to make *maamoul.* After all, Easter is only around the corner, and this is a very important recipe for all kinds of celebrations.' (*Maamoul*, Greta, is a Middle Eastern biscuit – pastry that is yummy and flaky and buttery.)

'Passed down from your mother?' I asked.

Nene nodded. 'And from her mother to her,' she said.

I imagined how far back this tradition went on my dad's side of the family, of generations of women sharing their recipes after growing up in a small village, surviving the deserts of Turkey, and even further back, from when there's no records other than stories that Nene remembers of how my ancestors lived.

Nene brought bowls of ingredients to the dressed table. Chopped walnuts and dates. And a bowl covered with plastic wrap that had a large ball of dough sitting in its well.

'*Maamoul* is a two-day recipe,' Nene said, pulling the dough out of the bowl. 'You mix your semolina, cinnamon, sugar and the shortening together with your fingers, like this,' she said, flexing her fingers. 'Then you leave it to sit in the fridge overnight, so it binds together into this dough.'

And using Nene's pre-prepared *maamoul* dough, Annie and I spent the rest of the afternoon moulding and rolling it into small biscuits. We made small rings, one of the traditional shapes. Sometimes, we pushed the date and walnut filling into the middle.

Nene even had a special instrument. It's like a wavy knife, but not sharp. 'You take the *ma'lat*, and you decorate,' she said, pressing the instrument into the edges of each biscuit, creating a wavy pattern. She then whisked away the tray of biscuits and slid it into the oven.

'I wish I'd filmed that,' Annie said.

'Already thought of that,' I said. I'd sneakily set my phone to time-lapse and placed it on the windowsill. The Food Fair taught me to make notes of our times in the kitchen, especially with

Nene, and I already wanted to share this recipe with Sami, Anh and Ha-na.

While we waited for the biscuits to cook, we sat at Nene's table and talked – about how Annie is planning to change the world using her genius ideas and computer skills (much of which I didn't understand . . .). About how happy Nene is to be home and healthy, although she did admit that she missed us all, too, and is excited that she gets to see us again in a few days for Easter. And then she pulled out the big guns – the dyed Easter eggs that we play games with. Those dyed eggs will sit alongside our decorated Ukrainian eggs at home, symbols of all the different threads of my family's history.

And I told them about my exciting idea, the one that I am planning for Friday . . .

It will be time to tell you about it really soon, Greta. But for now, I just have to send some other emails before I go to bed.

Bye for now,
Alice

SAVE FILE TAB 63

Alice Boghosian

Class 6O – Library writing project

Friday 2 April 2021

Dear Greta,

When I look back on it, it's amazing how it came together. I woke up feeling sick with nerves. But I checked my messages again from the night before, and everyone had replied and committed to it, so I couldn't exactly back out . . .

Maybe, when something *feels* right and that taking action is something you *must* do, it's easier to go forward with your plans. Because there is a goal in sight, and so you don't have time to worry about other things . . .

When I got to the school gate, it looked like a normal morning. Then I saw Ha-na and Sami, lurking at the gate, looking conspiratorial.

In fact, as we walked into the quadrangle, it looked like the whole of Year Six had turned up.

Jayden came towards me. 'The drone's inside,' he said, glancing at his watch. 'We've got ten minutes to get everyone ready – let's get the plan underway?'

I nodded while returning Jayden's high-five, and noticed Mrs Malouf walk into the playground just as Jayden disappeared into the school. Today, her brooch was a badge in the shape of a whale. Inside the whale was the word *Greenpeace.*

'I wore this for good luck,' she whispered, tapping her whale badge.

I couldn't help it – I gave my library teacher a quick hug! Nope, not bizarre at all, Greta . . . but it was that kind of day.

'Right, everyone,' I yelled. 'Time to move into formation! First lines go here,' and I pointed to Sami, who waved to the students.

'Second line HERE!' I pointed to Ha-na, whose hair was tucked behind her ears so her smile beamed for us all to see.

I was relieved when Ms O'Rourke brought some more kids from the younger years and organised them into place – yep, all the teachers were on board enacting the Alice Plan, and it felt fantastic! And, it freed me up to check that everyone was moving into the right places, just as we'd planned.

But then, I noticed something. Someone. Someone familiar, walking across the playground. And that's when my heart stopped. This was no belated April Fool's joke.

Walking across the playground, with Cortez by her side, was a very familiar figure. A very *real* figure. Not a robot.

I'm pretty sure I squealed.

'Wouldn't miss a protest for the world,' Anh said. 'Or for Greta! Or for my crew.'

I threw myself at her in the most gentle way I could.

'This is your two-minute call!' Cortez's voice burst through the loudspeaker. This was it . . .

I walked to the middle of the group, where everyone had taken their places – as planned in minute detail by Sami and me. Next to me, Jayden was holding the drone remote, lifting it higher and higher into the air, just like we'd planned.

Somewhere overhead, the drone was flying, rising up to take a snapshot of Melwood Public's *Fridays 4 Future* protest!!!

'It's time, Alice,' Jayden said.

'We're here because we care about our future,' I said, shakily. It sounded wobbly and weak over the portable PA system, and the microphone wavered in my hand. Cortez had shown me how to use it – now was the time to make sure my voice was clear – but I was having a hard time swallowing!

'Louder, Alice,' Jayden said, next to me.

'WE'RE HERE BECAUSE WE CARE ABOUT OUR FUTURE,' I said, more loudly into the microphone, and my voice sprang out crisp and clear. It took a beat, but suddenly a cheer rose up around the quadrangle.

I felt a surge of energy kick right through me, from my toes to the tips of my out-there curls. (Annie would be proud of me and my hair today.)

I looked at Jayden and nodded. Together, we lifted up the huge sign between us. I still can't believe that Jayden helped me paint it after I told him about my idea. I have to admit, I couldn't have done it without him.

‘Ready, Greta?’ Jayden joked above the raucous whoops and cheers.

And I was. In that moment, I was the most ready I’ve ever been . . .

Later, the drone shot proved how good it all looked.

FRIDAYS 4 FUTURE
SAVE THE PLANET
SAVE OUR GREEN AND GOLDEN BELL FROGS IN MELWOOD, SYDNEY, AUSTRALIA

The sign, in the middle of all of us students in Melwood.

Great idea, Greta.

Let’s save this planet together. 🤗

Alice

PS – I’m just about done tagging you in our photos so you can check it out for yourself!
PPS – I’m also going to tag my new friend @Peter @BrekkyHQ, too!
PPPS – I’m also going to tag Queenie Q, ya know, just in case.

SAVE FILE TAB 64

Alice Boghosian

Class 6O - Library writing project

Saturday 3 April 2021

Dear Greta,

Annie just came rushing into my room, jumping on the bed, smothering me in bedclothes. I wrenched my eyes open. Yep, still *my* bedroom, with *my* pink desk and *my* dirty clothes thrown across *my* chair . . . (But I miss Nene being here!)

Annie was wild with excitement, her curls springing up and out of her head, surely mirroring mine.

'Alice! ALICE! Wake up!' she cried in a frenzy. For a moment, I thought she might be having a heart attack (not that any heart problems are funny, but you know what I mean . . .).

'It's six seventeen in the morning,' I croaked.

'You did it, you did it, you did it! OH MY GOD!'

Annie peeled back the covers and thrust her phone under my face. It was the photo from our *Fridays 4 Future* protest yesterday, which I'd put on social media and everyone in our team had shared. Jayden had caught the best drone shot of our Year Six class forming the letters and numbers F 4 F in the playground. The shot went viral around everyone who was linked to the school. Just as I'd hoped and planned. To get Dad's frogs a little more attention. To hopefully save the wetlands, too.

'I've seen it,' I mumbled, wanting to get my last few snatches of sleep.

'It's not that . . . Look at *who* posted it,' Annie urged.

And so I looked at the photo again. *Really* looked at it.

Below our photo are hundreds, no, *thousands*, of new messages. Thousands of heart emojis. Thousands of frog emojis. So many hashtags.

#melwood #savethefrogs #sydney #australia
#greenandgoldenbellfrog #Fridays4future
#schoolstrikeforclimate #climatestrike

The messages are from people from around the world, learning about a little place called Melwood in Australia. And about the Green and Golden Bell Frog, too.

Thank you, Greta, for the re-tweet.

Your support means the world.

Lots and lots of love,
Alice

LEARN MORE

Would you like to learn more about Greta Thunberg? Here are some great resources that I used while researching this book.

Social media

Twitter and Instagram

Greta Thunberg: @GretaThunberg

Fridays 4 Future: @Fridays4Future

Books

No one is too small to make a difference, by Greta Thunberg, Penguin Books, 2019

I know this to be true: Greta Thunberg on truth, courage and saving our planet, by Geoff Blackwell, Murdoch Books, 2020

Little People, Big Dreams: Greta Thunberg, by Maria Isabel Sanchez Vegara, Frances Lincoln Children's Books, 2020

Film

I am Greta, Director: Nathan Grossman, B-Reel Films, 2020

Web

Greta Thunberg: Time's Person of the Year 2019, *Time* https://time.com/person-of-the-year-2019-greta-thunberg/

ACKNOWLEDGEMENTS

I would like to thank my inspiring friends at Technology 4 Learning in the NSW Department of Education for their support, namely Joachim, Heather, (the real) Anh, Krysta, Jacob, Greig, Linda and Mark. Many of the ideas in this book are taking place in real life, thanks to the remarkable innovations of this team.

Thank you to those legends who donated their names to the book: Anh Ha and Kat O'Rourke.

To my cheer squad – thank you Sue, Mandy, Susanne, Jacqui, Sarina and Zoe. Special thanks go to Beth for being the earliest champion of this story.

To the team at Penguin Random House – your warmth, expertise and guidance have been beacons!

To my family: Meg, Boghos, Camille, Martin, Charl, Louise, Daisy, Gracie, Harry and Efo, and to the memory of my powerhouse grandmothers: Vartouhi and Marjorie – *oudem.*

Finally, thank you, Greta, for not just being the inspiration for this book, but also providing a manifesto on how to approach the world at any age.

ABOUT THE AUTHOR

Yvette Poshoglian is the author of over forty books for children and young people, including the bestselling Ella and Olivia series. Born and raised in Sydney, Yvette taught secondary English in southwest Sydney and now manages major education projects for the NSW Department of Education. Currently she works at the intersection of pedagogy, technology and innovation with the Technology 4 Learning team at the NSW Department of Education. Many of the STEM and technology developments occurring in schools around NSW are captured in *Dear Greta*. Yvette has loads in common with her character Alice Boghosian, apart from Alice's horrible nickname.